Verney L. Cameron

Our Future Highway

in Two Volumes - Vol. 2

Verney L. Cameron

Our Future Highway
in Two Volumes - Vol. 2

ISBN/EAN: 9783348054072

Printed in Europe, USA, Canada, Australia, Japan

Cover: Foto ©Andreas Hilbeck / pixelio.de

More available books at **www.hansebooks.com**

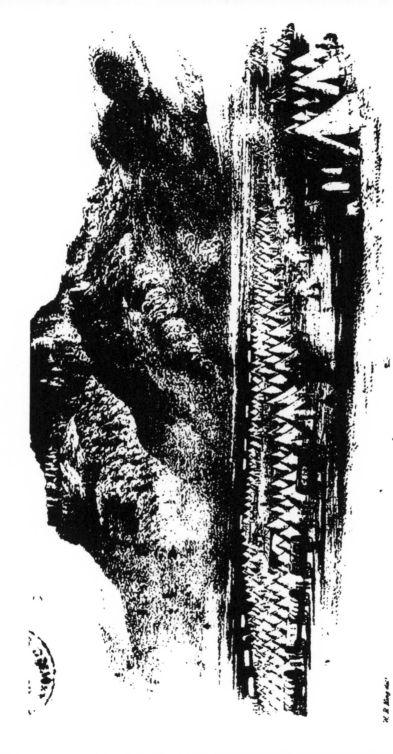

CAMP UNDER THE AMATOLAS.

OUR FUTURE HIGHWAY.

Our Future Highway.

BY

VERNEY LOVETT CAMERON, C.B., D.C.L.,

COMMANDER ROYAL NAVY,

Medallist of Royal, Paris. Lisbon Geo. Soc., of Soc. of Arts; Corresponding Member of Paris, Lyons, Norman. Italian, French Commercial, Belgian, Antwerp. Brussels, Berlin. Vienna. Hungarian Geo. Soc.; Member of Committee of International Geo. and Com. Soc F R G S F S A M A I F ~ His Soc ~

TWO VOLUMES.—VOL. II.

London:

MACMILLAN AND CO.

1880.

CONTENTS.

CHAPTER III.

·CHAPTER IV.

CONTENTS.

CHAPTER XV.

ILLUSTRATIONS.

CHAPTER I.

Shaykh Abed—Aneizeh—True nomads—Coffee—Circassians—The Sultan's message—The Shaykh's reply—Yuzbashi Erat—Impunity in evil-doing—Relations in the desert—Unbearable — Reduced to pauperism — Consular intervention — Consultation over — Spiked things — The coffee-maker—A master of the art—A curious party—*Barr-el-Soudan*—Tobacco-pouches—Beautiful scene—The sounds of revelry — "Tented fields" — True to his word — His favourite mare—No kill—Shoot for the pot—Ruins of Hierapolis—The ire of the Arabs—Three hundred priests—Equally futile — Five kettah for two cartridges—A medical levée—A huge bonfire —Target practice—Mixed bag—A swan—A miss fire—Packs of kettah—A dispute—Trust to myself—The right road—Go on — Hockey — Caverns — "Blue-rocks" — Emerging from a valley—A glowing report.

LIKE many of his followers Shaykh Abed, chief of the Arab camp, was a very favourable specimen of the semi-nomad. Indeed his people had only begun agriculture thirty years before, when they were forced to settle down at Mombedj by the Turkish Government as a guarantee for the

behaviour of the rest of the Aneizeh tribe, to
which they claimed to belong.   Most probably
there was something behind this story, for all
the Arabs look upon the purely nomad existence as the most gentlemanlike and aristocratic
and despise agriculture; naturally, therefore,
Shaykh Abed and his people liked to claim
relationship with one of the greatest and most
powerful of Arab clans, and to describe their
agriculture as being only subsidiary to their
pastoral pursuits.

They were still all living in tents of precisely
the same pattern as the true nomads, and,
though not making the great migrations which
the latter do, occasionally changed their location
to find more food or water for their flocks
and herds, but always made the Mombedj
their head-quarters, and occupied the same
place at seed-time and harvest.

When all was arranged, tents pitched and
horses and mules stabled under the Shaykh's
large tent, one side of which was open, we
assembled there, round a fire, for the inevitable

.coffee and talk. ˆShaykh Abed, who was a
fine handsome man of about five and thirty,
said he just remembered the settling down
of his father ᶜat Mombedj, and that since
that time all had gone well with them until
the Circassians were told to take up their
habitation there also. Whilst he was speaking
about this some Circassians came strolling in
and had to be invited to sit down and join in
the coffee-drinking ; this prevented for the time
any further confidences. The conversation
changed from the Circassians to shooting and
hunting, and the Shaykh, who possessed a
brace of very handsome black and white
greyhounds, said that if we would stop the
next day he would go out with us after gazelle,
when we could take our own dogs as well as his
and some others that were in the camp. The
Circassians said that their headman wanted
very much to see us, and we therefore told
them that if he would send to us in the
morning and say whether he would come to
us or we should go to see him we should be

glad to have a talk with him. When the
Circassians went away the Shaykh said that
he would come into our tent and tell us all
about his grievances, as people would be
always coming and going in his large one
so that we could not talk quietly there. We
accordingly moved over with two or three men
who were more in his confidence than the
rest, and he opened his mind very fully.

Before the Circassians had come to Mombedj
he had received a message that the Sultan
wished them to settle there, and that as they
were Mohammedans who had been driven
out of their homes by the common enemy
he hoped they would be kindly received.
They were to be allowed to build a village
in the ruins, and to pasture their cattle near,
and also to cultivate ground, but were not
to interfere with any that was already cultivated
by the Arabs. He replied that they should
be welcome, and that he and his people would
assist them to the best of his power. The
Circassians — when they arrived — were not

content with the land given them to cultivate, and tried to take that of the Arabs;
and when the latter objected broke their
ploughs and drove them, and prevented them
cultivating any land at all. An officer, Yuzbashi Erat, had been named to settle and
arrange all disputes between the Arabs and
Circassians, but seemed to have neglected his
duty wofully. He had left the place soon
after the Circassians arrived, and when the
Arabs sent in to him at Aleppo, had promised
to come out directly after *Bairam.* More
than six weeks had elapsed since then, and
though the Arabs had sent many messages
to him and a petition to the Wali imploring
his presence, no notice had been taken of their
appeals. The Circassians, through impunity
in evil-doing, were growing bolder, and now
were constantly stealing cattle and sheep, and
had even set upon women and children collecting brushwood for firing, and beaten and
robbed them. Shaykh Abed said that this
state of affairs could go on no longer, and

that when we arrived he had been on the
point of starting for Aleppo himself to see if
his own presence would have any influence on
the Wali; if that failed his intention was to
seek assistance from other Arabs and his relations in the desert and drive the Circassians
away by force.   The superior arms of the latter
had hitherto prevented the Arabs from taking
the law into their own hands, but, as the Shaykh
said, matters were becoming unbearable, and
that, though the Circassians were the better
armed, numbers would be on the side of the
Arabs, and even if they did lose many men
it would be better than putting up with matters
as they stood then.

We strongly urged him not to resort to
force, as it would put him and his people in
the wrong, and that even if they did overcome
the Circassians there were enough soldiers at
Aleppo to put him and all he could bring down
easily; in which case, instead of being rich
and prosperous, they would be reduced to
pauperism, as the troops would be sure to

take all their cattle and sheep away from them, so that they would have to depend entirely on the land for their support, while the Circassians, instead of being merely unpleasant neighbours, would develop into tyrannical masters.

Our advice was that he should represent his case to the consular body at Aleppo and pray for their intervention, and we promised to write to Henderson on the subject and inclose a statement drawn up by himself and his principal men as to the causes of their dissatisfaction with the Circassians. This letter he could send in at once to Aleppo; and we promised that if Henderson should meet us at Jerablus, as he had promised to do if possible, we would send over a messenger to let him know, so that he might have a personal interview with him.

Our consultation being over, we ordered supper to be brought, and asked the Shaykh to join; he said he had also had supper cooked for us, and proposed, as a compromise, that we should eat ours first and then send for

his and eat that. We first had ours served
in European fashion, with a table and seats.
The Shaykh and one of his friends who stayed
with him managed very fairly with knives and
forks, though they had never seen them used
before, and as we afterwards heard they could
not make out the reason why we wanted spiked
things to put our food in our mouths when
fingers were so much more handy. When
our supper was done the table was cleared
away and the Shaykh's produced, when we
had to squat down on the ground and conform
to the Arab manner of eating, the Shaykh
arguing, plausibly enough, that as we had made
him eat like a European it was only fair that
we should now eat like Arabs.

After this double-barrelled supper we went
back to the Shaykh's large tent, in the centre
of which was a fire of brushwood and where a
number of his people were assembled. The
coffee-maker, who occupied the principal place
in the circle, was an adept in his art, roasting
the berries to the exact point required, then

pounding them in his mortar with a sort of
rythmical cadence of the blows of the pestle,
occasionally allowing some aspiring youth to
imitate his performance, but always being dis-
satisfied and resuming the duty himself. The
coffee being pounded, he paid the greatest attention to boiling the water, putting in the coffee
and pouring it from pot to pot, ere it was pronounced fit for use ; then a delicate rinse of the
cups with the smallest possible drop of the precious fluid ; and at last, having first tasted the
brew himself, the exactitude with which he
poured it into the tiny cups out of which it
was to be drunk ; all these were done with the
precision and grace of a master of the art.

The coffee, when made, certainly repaid the
pains bestowed on its making, and the services
óf the artist were in demand during the whole
evening. A curious party it seemed, all squatting and sprawling about on carpets and
cushions, the Shaykh and ourselves in the
centre, and conversation about all things,
from sport to war ; questions about railways,

telegraphs, English horses, dogs, guns, houses ;
how it was possible to live in a country where
there was no sun ; in fact all sorts of questions
both absurd and sensible, ranging from the
wildest vagaries of "the thousand and one
nights" to the most prosaic details of the
nineteenth century. All were eager to know
about Africa, and were delighted to hear that
Arabs were the most adventurous and successful
of merchants in the *Barr-el-Soudan,* and that
I had lived with and made friends with Arabs
in those far-distant lands. They could hardly,
however, understand how Arabs managed to
exist in a country where they had neither
camels nor horses, and protested that they
would prefer to remain poor in their own land
to get rich in one where they would have to
make painful journeys on foot. Our tobacco
pouches were freely indented on by our friends,
as the tobacco they grew for themselves or
bought in small towns or villages was not so
good in their opinion as ours, which we had
brought from Aleppo.

The scene was very beautiful; out in the clear cold moonlight stood our white tent glistening in the rays, flocks of sheep and herds of cattle clustering round the black tents of their owners, and in the centre the circle of Arabs in their picturesque dresses, the hanging *kofia* or handkerchief which they wear on their heads heightening the wild look of their features, alternately in brilliant light or deep shade as the fire blazed up when fresh brush-wood was added, and then died down again to a mere heap of mouldering embers.

It was nearly midnight ere we broke up, and the sounds of revelry continued some time longer in another tent where our servants and muleteers had been making merry with some of the Arabs. Songs and dancing had been going on uninterruptedly ever since eight o'clock, and had not ceased when we went to sleep. Although Arab music is very different from the European idea of harmony, and in a house or room is abominable to most civilised ears; still here, in " tented fields," the wild choruses seem to have a spirit and a swing, and are not destitute of a rude harmony which is particularly appropriate to the surroundings.

The Shaykh, true to his word, had his horses and dogs ready in the morning, and after an early breakfast we went out to look for gazelle. We had not been long away before we saw a herd of nearly forty, and got up to within about fifty yards before they saw us; we slipped the dogs, six in all, as they started; but it was a case of an *embarras de richesses*, as the grey-hounds were confused and kept on changing. However we had a delightful gallop, and scattered the herd into small groups of three and four each. After half-an-hour of galloping we pulled up to collect the dogs again, and I got off to let my horse Sultan have a rest, as he had been hard worked the day before. Whilst I was standing by his side two gazelle came over the crest of a hill close by, and away swept the Arabs and dogs after them; as I tried to mount the saddle turned round, and Sultan was so excited that it was ten minutes ere I could girth it up again and remount. He seemed to enjoy the fun just as much as any of us, and when we had another run shortly afterwards, passed the whole field, though the Shaykh did his utmost to hold his own on his favourite mare.

We had no kill, though several gazelle had shaves, and after a bit the greyhounds got so beat that it was no use going on. Indeed it is very rare indeed that a greyhound can run down a gazelle unless he can get within twenty yards or so before he is slipped, and at this season of the year, January, when the gazelle are in good condition for going, the only chance the dogs have is after heavy rain, when the small feet of the gazelle sink into the mud, and they can get no resistance to spring from.

When we got back to the tents Schaefer went out shooting, and I lent my gun to Elias the cook to shoot for the pot, whilst I rode over on Count to have a look at the ruins and to see why the Circassians had not sent over to arrange about their headman's visit.

The ruins of Hierapolis are clearly visible, parts of the walls still standing, and in some places being nearly forty feet high ; lines of streets may be traced, as also of aqueducts, and small reservoirs may be seen, besides the large one into which the subterranean canal discharges its waters. The stone of which it was built is a yellowish fossiliferous limestone, the same stone as is used in Aleppo at the present day ; and though there were not any great architectural remains there was enough to prove that in ancient days it had been a prosperous and well-built town. Two small mosques mark the burial-places of some Mohammedan santons, and the Circassians had raised the ire of the Arabs by violating these ; as, although not fanatical or austere in their religion, indeed very often so lax as to neglect prayers and rites altogether, the Arabs pay a great respect to the memory of the dead, and could not understand the Circassians, who were

said to be of the same religion as themselves, desecrating spots which they held in
veneration.

Hierapolis is famous as the point where
Julian the Apostate collected the armies which
he destined to overturn the empire of Sapor,
the representative of Sassanian monarchy. It
possessed at one time a magnificent temple,
whose rich endowments supported three hundred
priests in ease and luxury. The term "*Ninus
vetus*" used by Ammianus seems to give some
authenticity to an idea that it was once a seat
of the Assyrian monarchy, and perhaps had
somewhat to do with its identification with
Karchemish, which has been upset by Mr.
Smith's discoveries.

Now all that is to be seen are the ruins and
the square huts of the Circassians, into whose
village I rode after having been round the ruins;
I tried in vain to find any one who could, or
would, understand me, and my search for their
chief or the man whom I had seen the previous
evening was equally futile, so that I was obliged

to come away without hearing their side of the story in their disputes with the Arabs.[1]

Disappointed in this I rode back to our tent, where I found Schaefer had had very good sport, having shot several snipe and teal, whilst Elias, by crafty and pot-hunting tactics, had secured five kettah for two cartridges.

The rest of the afternoon passed away in a medical *levée*, and if I was not able to relieve all who applied to me, I was able favourably to impress others by the power of my remedies. Ophthalmia was very prevalent, and I had to treat both children in arms and toothless old greybeards for it. The favourite remedy of the Arabs for ophthalmia is pounded sugar-candy, which they call English sugar, distinguishing it from Zuka-al-Mesr, or Egyptian sugar, which they only use for eating, and of which they are

---

[1] Some time afterwards I heard from Henderson that Shaykh Abed had been in to see him at Aleppo, and that things had been going on from bad to worse until they had culminated in the Circassians murdering an Arab. Henderson had taken up the cause of the Arabs, and was in hopes that the Circassians would be removed from the neighbourhood of Mombedj.

inordinately fond. I was prayed to restore the paralytic to health, to remove the blame of sterility from women, and if I had no medicines which would have the desired effect, to write charms which they might wear, and which would by time and faith bring about the wished-for result.

Our evening passed in much the same way as the previous one, and it was again late before we got to bed. One feature in the night's entertainment was a huge bonfire in the open space in front of the Shaykh's tent, around which there was a great dance and song, between fifty and sixty men joining in it; it was a weird performance, and both to eye and ear a very impressive one.

Next morning we sent on our mules as soon as they were loaded, and stopped to have a final talk with the Shaykh. Just before we started he expressed a wish to be allowed to fire off my Winchester, which he had been attentively examining. I let him do so, and then he wanted to see me fire at something, so after

C

a bit we selected a large white stone about a
hundred and fifty yards off, at which I fired the
whole twelve cartridges as fast as I could, and
luckily did not miss once.   The Shaykh then
tried, but could not manage it at all, the only
weapon he was acquainted with being the
lance.   With many warm good-byes, and amidst
invitations to return and stay with him for as
long as we chose, and whenever we chose, we at
last parted from the Shaykh, and rode on after
our caravan.

As we were riding along we kept on flushing
snipe and duck from a stream that ran close
by the track, and I determined when we got
up to the animals to let my horse be led, and
walk along the bank with my fowling-piece,
and try for a mixed bag, nor was I disappointed.

Walking close to the stream, I was constantly
getting shots at snipe and teal, and occasionally
at big duck of varying kinds; and in one place
I had a great piece of good fortune.   I saw
some large duck swimming on an open piece

in the stream, and tried to get up to them
for a shot. Before I could get near enough
to fire they got up and skirred across a rise
which hid the next bend of the stream from
us. Growling at my luck, I crept up the near
side of the slope, and not only saw my ducks,
but also a swan. The latter was standing,
wrapt in meditation, about a hundred yards
from the nearest place where I could get under
cover. I slowly and stealthily went back till
I could stand upright, and then signing to the
caravan to remain still and quiet, I rushed to
my horse and took the Winchester from the
saddle. I then retraced my steps, and was
all anxiety as I reached the slope to know if
when I was able to peer over again the swan
would still be there. As I gently raised my
head, I again saw him, but he had shifted his
position somewhat, which made approaching
him more difficult than it was before, but by
creeping on hands and knees along an irrigation
cut, and taking advantage of sedges and grasses
growing on its edge, I was able to get to within

about ninety yards.   I raised myself, cautiously,
put the hammer to full cock gently, so as not to
make a click, took a steady aim and pressed the
trigger : snap went the striker on the cartridge,
but no report; the cartridge had missed fire.
To bring the next into action was the work
of a second, but my beautiful bird was alarmed,
and was twisting about, flapping his wings, and
hopping away just as if he was going to take
flight.   Whether to fire at him on the move, or
to wait on the chance of his stopping again, was
difficult to decide.   I luckily kept as still as a
stock or a stone, and he settled down quietly
about fifteen yards further away.   Again I drew
a bead on him and pressed the trigger : was it
to be another miss-fire or not ?   Hurrah! there
was a bang and a kick, and the swan rolling
over in his death agony.   I rushed out after
him, getting up to my middle in mud and slime;
but it did not matter, I had got him, and bore
him back in triumph to Elias, into whose charge
I consigned him.   Besides the wild-fowl I also
got some kettah and francolin, and altogether

in about three hours' tramp got somewhere about forty head of mixed game—a very good day's wild sport, the bag varying in size from a snipe to a swan.

At last we came to the Nahr Sadschur, into which the stream we had been following fell, and which the path to Jerablus crossed. Here I washed off the mud and dirt with which I was covered, and got on my horse again. We now began to go over bleak hill sides covered with small brush which much reminded one of heather on the Scottish mountains, and here the kettah were packed in enormous quantities. Neither Schaefer nor I cared much to go after them, as we had still a good distance to go, and our gamebag was sufficiently full to supply our commissariat for some days. After some time the tracks diverged, and there was a dispute between the muleteers and Mohammed, the zaptieh, as to which was the right way; some shepherds whom we appealed to differed as to which line we should follow, so I determined to

trust to myself. Knowing that the Euphrates
must be in sight from some hills on our
right, I rode off to the top of the highest
to see if I could pick up any points near
Jerablus which I might recognise. On arriving there I saw the river and the hills opposite
Jerablus, so rode down, waving to the caravan
to come to me. In a short time an intervening hill hid them from my sight, and
when I struck the line down which I intended
them to come, I got off, and knee-haltering
my horse, sat down for a smoke. After waiting some time, Daher and one of the servants
came down, saying that a man had told
Schaefer the right road, and that he and
the caravan were following it. I was not
inclined to go back, so told the two and
Gabriel, who also came up a few minutes
after, to come with me along the line I had
chosen. We soon got into a sort of ravine
leading down between two hills to the plain
of the river. In this ravine was a large
Arab encampment, and on a piece of level

ground at its mouth all the young men and
boys were playing hockey. Once on the
plain we rode along under the shadow of
the cliffs which divide the hilly from the
level portion. These cliffs are soft limestone
and numberless caverns are cut in their faces.
Some of these are now inaccessible, others are
partly fallen in ; but a good number are inhabited by the poorer Arabs, who with their
cattle find a warm and dry shelter in these
ancient caves. Besides these troglodytes,
pigeons and martens innumerable had their
nest in the cliffs, and I could not resist the
temptation of potting a couple of " blue
rocks " with my carbine as they were sitting
on the top of the cliffs sunning themselves
in the evening sun. Though the accuracy
of the carbine was proved the poor birds
were uselessly sacrificed, as the bullets had
smashed them up so much that they were
unfit for food. As we came out from under
the shadow of the cliffs and the plain widened
out we could just see Jerablus in the distance,

and at the same moment firing from the caravan drew my attention to it emerging from a valley in the hills.

I galloped across to them and pointed out Jerablus, so that they might steer straight for it. Though in sight of Jerablus at sunset, it was not reached till nearly two hours later, as darkness closing in on us compelled us to pick our way carefully for fear of holes made by jerboa rats and the rootings of wild pigs.

When we did arrive, everybody turned out to welcome us, and Shaykh Hosayn put the same house at our disposal that I had occupied on our previous visit. This we now made into stable and kitchen, and pitched our tents for our own lodging.

Raschid made his appearance with a glowing report of how he had been working and how much he had done, but we were all tired, and deferred business and conversation to the morning.

CHAPTER II.

IN the morning when we had got matters
settled I sent for Raschid in order to find out
how he had been getting on with the digging.
Very well indeed, was his answer; but on
further inquiry I found that only three and

a half days' work had been done since I left
nearly three weeks before.   Some more stones
with hieroglyphics on them had been found
near the two large bas-reliefs, and between the
latter was a flight of steps.

Next morning we first went over to the
ruins and set the people to work again.   The
bas-relief which had not been broken had two
figures of men standing on a crouching lion,
the hinder one of whom carried an axe, and the
other two large feather fans, their hair and beards
being arranged something after the Assyrian
fashion.   The steps were broad and shallow, and
the stones with the hieroglyphics on them
seemed to have formed the sides of the entrance
into whatever place the steps led ; below the bas-
reliefs was a foundation of large rough stones,
and it seemed as if during the existence of the
more modern town the building of which these
stones formed part had been partially thrown
down and other edifices erected above the
remains.

The men being once more fairly at work, we

went on to the islands to look for pig, but
had no luck, although we went up the river to
the island where I had turned out fourteen,
and rode through and through the scrub in
which they had been lying on the previous
occasion. Enormous flocks of starlings were
roosting on small trees which grew in places
on the face of the bank of the river, and numbers
of pelicans and other water-fowl were swimming
on its breast as we rode back in the evening.

Raschid made an excuse for not having
worked more during my absence, saying that
Shaykh Hosayn had interfered with him. When
we sent for the Shaykh about this he said that
the Kaimacan at Bir-ed-jik had sent down to
know why he had permitted the digging to
go on, and whether he was to be paid anything for it. The Shaykh said he had been
paid nothing, and thought the message of the
Kaimacan a good opportunity to try and get
something out of us. He had a friend called
Hajji Schalbach, a merchant at Bir-ed-jik,
stopping with him, who chimed in vague

complaints against the Kaimacan, but when we
urged both to give us some definite idea of
what the acts of which they complained were,
they declined, saying that if anything were done
to the Kaimacan in consequence of their complaints, and it was known that they had furnished
information, the successors of the present man
would, even if he were impotent, cause them
great annoyance and trouble for having dared
to report the doings of an official.   Hajji
Schalbach was a large proprietor, owning several
villages near Bir-ed-jik, and was strongly in
favour of commuting the tithes for a fixed
money payment, as under the present system
more loss is caused to the owners by the
grain not being garnered until measured by
the tithe collector than the amount of the
tithe itself.   The *corvée*, he said, fell heavily
on his peasantry, at which old Hosayn laughed,
and said that the government knew better than
to attempt to come out to his and the surrounding villages to get men for *corvée*, as they
would be driven away, but that their camels

and mules were often taken when they were in towns, and that months often passed without his knowing where the animals were.

Both Shaykh Hosayn and the Hajji had supper with us and sat up long after talking and smoking, and the Shaykh, waxing bold as the evening went on, challenged me to a race for a pound: I was to ride Sultan, and he his mare. This challenge I accepted at once for the fun of the thing, and it was arranged to come off next morning.

Soon after we were up in the morning Shaykh Mohammed and a friend of his, Shaykh Murad, came over to see us, and promised to stop and see the race, and afterwards have luncheon with us. When I sent for Shaykh Hosayn to arrange about the distance and direction in which we were to ride, he was not to be found, having started before daylight with his friend Schalbach for Bir-ed-jik.

After visiting the ruins we followed the advice of Daher, that "*Massu allaient autre voyage en Bapor*," which being interpreted meant that we

should send some men across to the other side
of the river to drive the pigs out of their lairs in
some valleys and ravines there, and make them
come over to our side.   After a little bother
we got half-a-dozen to go in a primitive ferry-
boat fashioned something like an over-grown
packing-case with sloping ends, and they did
manage to drive one pig across.   Schaefer
wounded him soon after he landed on our
side, and then he swam to another island which
was on the other side of an unfordable branch
of the stream, where he lay down close to some
cattle, so that we did not dare to fire at him.
Neither the herdsmen who were looking after
the cattle nor the men we had sent to drive the
pigs would understand our shouts and signals
to send him back towards us, and there he lay
for over an hour, and we had to go back to
our tent to entertain Shaykhs Mohammed and
Murad.   Elias had prepared an Arab meal;
and we all squatted down in company; whilst
we were eating who should appear but Shaykh
Hosayn, who had just returned from starting

his friend for Bir-ed-jik, and who was nothing
loth to join in when invited.

We all chaffed him very much about having
challenged me to ride a race and then going
away without leaving any word about it; after
a time he promised to ride the next morning,
and the course was to be from the village to
the ruins.   Shaykh Mohammed said he would
come over again to see the fun, and would send
a young mare of the Seglawi breed to join in,
but that as it was only to try her he would not
put any money on.

After luncheon was over we went to look
after our friend the wounded pig, but he had
gone; however, we turned up three which were
lying in the bush, and wounded one. As usual,
he went straight for the river and tried to swim
back to the other side; we kept up a hot fire on
him as he was swimming, and one bullet striking
him in the head finished his mortal career.   The
Massus who were coming back in the *Bapor*
(*bateau-à-vapeur* is, I suppose, the derivation of
the last word) tried to get his carcase, but they

couldn't manage it, owing to the unwieldiness of their craft.

Shaykh Mohammed wanted us very much to go and stay at his village, where he said we should be among real Arabs, and would not have to pay for anything however long we might choose to stop; whilst Shaykh Hosayn was half a Kurd or a Turk, and would make us pay for the use of his house, and for every egg, fowl, or grain of barley that we wanted. We could not very well comply with his request, so we compromised matters by promising to go over the next day and have dinner with him at two or three o'clock in the afternoon.

Schaefer and I knowing how tobacco usually went in these sort of visits, were rather loth to go, as our stock was getting low, and we were still bound to wait for a day or so more on the chance of Henderson turning up.

Some small pieces of broken stones and a fragment or two of glass were found to-day at the ruins, where we were only keeping a small

number of men at work, as the money for paying them had to be husbanded, and more
efficient supervision could be kept up over a
small than over a large number of workmen.

In the morning I got hold of Shaykh Hosayn,
who at first said he was not well, and could not
ride, and then that he would not ride for
money. Shaykh Mohammed, who came up at
this time, said he had heard him promise to
ride for a pound, and that he would be eternally
disgraced if he hauled off. He at last consented
to start for the race, but would not promise
about the money. It was all over with him
and his mare in less than two hundred yards,
but Shaykh Mohammed's mare was waiting
for me half way to the ruins, so I went on
to try her. About a hundred yards before I
got up, the man who was riding her set her
going, and it was five or six hundred yards
more before I could pass her. Sultan seemed
thoroughly to enjoy the fun, and was not a bit
distressed by a two-mile gallop. Schaefer, who
had been marking the point for the winning-

post, now rode back with me, and agreed that if
Shaykh Hosayn said he would not pay the
pound, I should chase him if he was still on his
horse, and get his cloak or *kofia* from him. He
and Shaykh Mohammed came to meet us, and
Shaykh Hosayn began to chaff and laugh,
saying that he had never intended that we
should ride a race. I appealed to Shaykh
Mohammed, and said that if I was not paid
I should have the cloak off Hosayn's back,
but that he might ride for it. Old Hosayn
thought at first I meant nothing; but at last
I got him to start, and although he managed
to twist and turn pretty well, I soon got hold
of his cloak, but it was too well tied on to
pull it off without tearing something; so, letting
go of his cloak, I put my arm round his waist,
and before he well knew where he was, had
him across my saddle. Everybody was shouting with laughter, in which the old Shaykh
himself joined, when I pulled up and let him
down to the ground, after telling him that both
he and his cloak now belonged to me.

This little lark being over, we went again
to the ruins, where they were still digging
near the bas-reliefs in line with the directions
in which they ran, to see if anything could be
found of the room or temple, the entrance of
which they had adorned. When this was done
it was time for us to go over to Ras Ali, to
lunch with Shaykh Mohammed. We soon
reached there and were welcomed into his tent,
the reception part of which was divided from
the women's quarters by a screen of reeds
fastened together by coloured worsted worked
into a pattern. All round were spread Persian
and Kurdish carpets, and silken cushions were
provided for us to lean upon. Our riding-
boots being rather in the way when squatting
on the ground, the Shaykh had them pulled
off, and then coffee and pipes were produced.
We had brought all our remaining stock of
tobacco with us, but when we produced it the
Shaykh and man who seemed to be his first
lieutenant, would not hear of our using our own
tobacco when on a visit to him, and filled our

pipes for us themselves; the only thing which they consented to, was that we should make a temporary exchange of pipes. After some time, during which we smoked and were plied with alternate cups of tea and coffee, food was brought in, Shaykh Mohammed who was a great dandy, did not have his bread, as was usually the case, shied down anyhow round the edges of the carpet on which the dishes were arranged, but it was neatly folded and arranged in a sort of pattern. We had pillau of rice and fowls, cheese, onions, honey, and stewed figs, all well cooked and clean. Amongst the guests was a full-blooded negro, who with one of the Arabs had been a prisoner of war, and had lately been released. They passed five months altogether with the Russians, and said they had not at all enjoyed the time; they used to be made to work, and if they refused were beaten with sticks. Their food was coarse and insufficient as a rule, but one day when some Englishmen were brought by Russian officers to see them, they had a red-letter day. When they were

freed at the termination of the war, the Russians
gave each man three piastres, and on arriving
in the Turkish lines they found no preparation
made for them. The greater part of the
prisoners were incorporated in some Turkish
regiments, which were on the spot when they
arrived, but these two and some twenty others
were sent to Constantinople, whence our friends
had made their way by begging to their own
homes, which they never wished to leave again
for the purpose of fighting. The Shaykh up-
braided them with want of patriotism, and said
if it were not that he was married, and had
to support his wives and children and his old
mother he would have volunteered for the war
himself.

Soon after sunset we returned to Jerablus,
and for once in a way got to bed in decent
time. Next day we had a *levée* of all the
sick for some miles round, and where we
thought we could do any good distributed
medicines and ointments to the applicants.
Others who were beyond our skill we

recommended to go in to the European doctors at Aleppo, but they did not seem to relish the prospect of having to pay to be cured; the general idea seeming to be that the doctor should not only prescribe and provide medicines, but that he should also feed and lodge his patients whilst under his care, and all without making any charge.

No news arriving about Henderson, we gave up all hopes of seeing him, and decided to wait no longer, but to start the next morning. When the morning arrived it was a nasty, cold, drizzly day, almost freezing, and our people were very dilatory in packing, trusting to something occurring to make us delay our departure another day. Notwithstanding the bad weather Shaykhs Mohammed and Murad and many of their people came over to wish us good-bye, and at last, at a quarter before eleven, we managed to make a start.

As we went along the rain gradually ceased, but was succeeded by a bitter cold wind from the north-east. We saw a few hares, but the weather was too wretched to do any coursing, and we were not sorry when at half-past two we came to a khan where we were able to get some hot coffee and bread, and warm ourselves round a blazing fire. Nearly all the people belonging to the village round the khan were away attending a marriage feast at a place a few miles off. The two or three who remained to look after the place were busy stripping the fibrous sheath off large reeds; this after being dressed they make into rope; the reeds when stripped were thrown on the fire and made a cheerful blaze.

Soon after we left the khan we could see the trees in the gardens around Bir-ed-jik, and shortly afterwards we could distinguish the castle, which is built of a very light reddish-yellow limestone; the houses, being all of chalk, and built against a very steep chalk hill, we could not distinguish till long after. As we got nearer the town we saw some men with grey-hounds stalking a few gazelle, amongst which was a black one, but they were some distance

from our road, and it was necessary to press on
if we were to reach the ferry in time to get
across to Bir-ed-jik that same evening.

At last we arrived on an expanse of level
ground which is covered by the river during
the spring floods, and cantered on to try to
get boats ready by the time the mules should
arrive. When we got opposite the town all
the boats had ceased plying, and the wind was
blowing furiously from the eastern shore so
that our shouting and firing of guns was for
a long time unnoticed. After some time we
attracted attention, and one of the nonde-
script craft put off and came lumbering across
the river.

Noah's ark must have been a Blackwall
clipper when compared with the machine that
was making its painful way towards us. She
was built of rough planks with clumsy ribs,
caulked with cotton and paid with bitumen.
Her floors were quite flat, and the sides stood
up at right angles to them ; the bow, or rather
the part that went first curved up slightly and

was quite open. The stern ran up into a high peak, on which was pivoted a huge paddle made of rough branches rudely joined together; at the outer end a piece of plank was nailed on and a large stone lashed on the inner one to act as a counterpoise. On a sort of platform stood the skipper and his mate, who used

FERRY BOAT.

this paddle to direct the course, and at intervals worked a pole to propel their vessel forwards; at the bow three men laboured, as with an oar, at a pole destitute of any blade, going through contortions and evolutions which would have driven any rowing men frantic. This oar was worked on the downstream side of the boat so

as to assist in keeping her head up. Of course
when they fetched our side they had drifted
a long way down and the crew had to get out
and track her up. The open bow just laid on
the bank, and we got our horses and some
of the mules, which had come up, on board
and started across. By the time we arrived
at the Eastern bank it had got quite dark
and the chief of the boatmen said it was against
orders for boats to cross the river at night.
There we were, a bitter cold wind blowing,
sleet falling, and no cook, and no beds. We
managed to get some coffee, and shelter our
horses in a café, but could find no lodging
for ourselves.

When we asked where the Kaimacan lived
we had great difficulty in getting any one to
show the way, as it was said to be too late to
disturb him. At last Mohammed, the zaptieh,
lit upon a corporal, and we sent Gabriel off
with them to see the Kaimacan and explain
our predicament. Gabriel returned in about
half an hour with two soldiers who had been

ordered to get boats to go across for our people. They were unable to get any one to go, and after three quarters of an hour of wrangling and fighting between them and the boatman we thought it best to go and see the Kaimacan ourselves.

We found a jolly-looking old gentleman sitting in a small room with a couple of friends. The greater part of the room was taken up by a stove and divans, chairs and cupboards, whilst on the wall hung a double barrelled breech-loader and a game bag.

We apologised for troubling him, but he said we were quite right, and sent off one of his companions to see about the boats and for a khan-keeper to arrange about our lodgings for the night. Our conversation was limited, as he only spoke Turkish and a very few words of French. However, we managed to get on very well, and as we waxed friendly he said he had something better than coffee for us to drink, and out of the game bag came a flask full of raki and from a cupboard was produced a bottle

—by the side of which a Jeroboam would have been a baby—full of Bir-ed-jik wine.

The old gentleman was jerkily polite, and kept hopping about and chirruping like a canary. Whilst we were there a telegram was brought in, and he first hopped for his seal and ink to stamp the receipt, then for his spectacles, and then for a candle to read it by, all the time saying, " *Télégramme*, ha, ha! *Télégramme*, ho, ho! *Télégramme*, hi, hi!" as if receiving a telegram was the best fun in the world. After some little stay with him we went away, and found the boats gone, and that Mohammed had gone with them; so we saw our horses stabled and fed in the café, and went up to the khan, where we found an unfortunate beggar being turned out of a square cell-like room, to make place for us, he having to go and chum with some one else. The khan-keeper got us some supper, and we awaited the arrival of the boats in peace. At last Mohammed returned, and said that he had found the people housed in a khan on the other side, having got tired of waiting on the river bank, and that the muleteers said that they were too tired to load up again ; so that he had to be content with bringing our sleeping sacks for us, which he had the good sense to think of.

We were soon sleeping the sleep of the tired, though our three selves, Schaefer, Gabriel and I, nearly filled up the available floor space, and our greyhounds—of which we now had three, having bought a white one called Saada at Jerablus—as usual, wanted the most comfortable corners.

Next day we got boats away betimes for our people, and as our tubs had not arrived went to the Turkish bath, which proved a very comfortable place on a cold wet day. Whilst in the hot room a fat old fellow came up and saluted us most warmly, and I could not make out who it was for some time, when it turned out to be Hajji Schalbach, whom I could scarcely recognise, the absence of clothes making such a difference in his personal appearance. Our people did not get over in time for us to make

a start forward, so we had to be content to
wait a day ; but now other travellers had left
the khan, and we got ample accommodation
rooms for sleeping and the servants, one for
sitting in, kitchen for the cook, and stables
for the horses, all under the same roof. Our
stay also gave us an opportunity of replenishing
our stores of sugar, tobacco, coffee, and other
small necessaries, which we had not had an
opportunity of doing since leaving Aleppo ;
and doing, a little mending in our wardrobes
and saddlery, so we resigned ourselves to it
contentedly.

CHAPTER III.

English merchants, Ralf Fitch—Sir Edward Osborne—Birra
—Feligia—A gun is very good—John Eldred—A dry
town—Maundrell—Bashaw of Urfa—Chesney—Travelling bad—A curious town—A mere shell—Large tents—
Caves—German sausage—Sport—Scouts the idea—A
curious instance — A wizard — Full confidence — A
samovar—Carts—A procession—The *Mustafiz*—Three
instead of two—Mohair goats—A wild looking fellow—
In the wars—A dispute—Robbers—Starts off running—
The most cowardly—Mock courage—Patrol—Quite
happy—Tsamelik—Wet and cold—Splash, splash, splash
—Smell smoke—Fear of robbers—A dreary scene—
Nimshi—Close proximity—Dull and gloomy—Weary
plodding—The Cadi—Orfa—Liquid mud—Pitchy darkness—The Serai—The Sergeant-Major—The Bimbashi
—An invitation.

BIR-ED-JIK, in the reign of Queen Elizabeth,
was well known to our English merchants, who
used to pass by there in their adventurous journeys to the Indies. Some used to take boat
at Bir-ed-jik and drift down the Euphrates;

others, "in order that they might sooner and
with less labour reach Bagdat," used to go by
Orfa to the Tigris. Though we may conjecture
that the boats they used were somewhat like
the ferry boats, and therefore not over easy to
navigate, still we can see from the precautions
taken by these pioneers of commerce that the
voyage was a difficult and dangerous one.

Several of these journeys are described by
those who took part in them and the following
extract from one may be of interest :—

"In the year of our Lord 1583 I, Ralf Fitch, of London,
merchant, being desirous to see the countries of the East
India, in the company of Mr. John Newberie, merchant,
(who had been at Ormuz once before,) of William Leeds,
jeweller, and James Storie, painter, being chiefly set forth
by the Right Worshipful Sir Edward Osborne,[1] knight, and
Mr. Richard Steper, citizens and merchants of London, did
ship myself in a ship of London, called the Tygre, wherein
we went for Tripolis, in Syria, and from thence we took
the way to Aleppo, which we went in seven days with the
caravan. Being in Aleppo and finding good company, we
went from thence to Birra, which is two days and a half travel

---

[1] His great grandson, Sir Thomas Osborne, when prime
minister, was made Earl of Danby by Charles II., and afterwards created Marquis of Carmarthen and Duke of Leeds,
by William of Orange.

with camels. Birra is a little town, but very plentiful of ·
victuals, and near to the walls of the town runneth the river
Euphrates. There we bought a boat and agreed with a
master and bargeman to go to Babylon; these boats to
be had but for one voyage, for the stream doth run so fast
downwards that they cannot return. They carry you to
a town, which they call Felugia, and then you sell the boat
for a little money; for that which cost you fifty at Birra you
will sell there for seven or eight. From Birra to Felugia
is sixteen days' journey; it is not good that one boat should
go alone, for if it should chance to break, you should have
much ado to save your goods from the Arabians, who will
always be thereabouts robbing, and in the night when
your boats are made fast it is necessary you should keep
good watch. For the Arabians, who are thieves, will
come swimming, and steal your goods, and flee away,
against which a gun is very good, for they fear it very much.
In the river of Euphrates, from Birra to Felugia, there are
certain places where you pay custom, so many medines
for a horse or camel's lading, and certain raisins and soap,
which is for the sons of Arbaries, who is lord of the
Arabians, and of all that great desert, and hath some
villages upon the river. Felugia, where you unload your
goods which come from Birra, is a little village from whence
you may go to Babylon in a day."

In 1583 John Eldred " with six or seven
other honest merchants" set sail from London.
They arrived at Tripoli where the English had
a consul and a factory called " *Fondeghi Inglis.*"
Then from Tripoli they went to Aleppo, which
was " the greatest place of traffic for a dry town,

that is in all these parts," and thence in three days to "Biresh." He said that the stream there was as "big as the Thames at Lambeth, and running almost as swift as the Trent." In twenty-eight days he arrived at Felugia and was then transported by donkeys to Baghdad, where they again took ship for "Bassora."

Maundrell in 1699 writes as follows :—

"April 20th. The river is here (Jerabolus) as large as the Thames at London; a long bullet gun could not shoot a ball over it, but it dropped in the river.

"April 22hd. We continued at our station (opposite Bir) not daring to cross the river for fear of falling into the hands of the chiah of the Bashaw of Urfa, who was at Bir, ordering many boats of corn down to Bagdad.

"April 23rd. The chiah being now departed, Sheik Assyne invited us over to Bir. We crossed in a boat of the country, of which they have a great many, this being the great pass into Mesopotamia. The boats are of a miserable fabric, flat and open in the fore part for horses to enter. They are large enough to carry about four horses each. Their way to cross is by drawing up the boat as high as they know to be necessary, and then with wretched oars striking over; she falls a good way down, by the force of the stream, before they arrive at the further side."

Chesney found at Bir-ed-jik sixteen ferry boats, and heard that the caravans sometimes amounted to five thousand camels.

Even in earlier days Bir was of great importance, as we find it repelling an attack made upon it by Sapor, the opponent of Julian the Apostate, who sought to seize it as commanding the passage of the Euphrates.

We ourselves found fifteen ferry boats, and although rain had rendered the travelling very bad, over five hundred camels crossed the river each way during the day we were there; and camped on the outskirts of the town were over a thousand more.

Maundrell's account is interesting as showing that the ferry boats in his time were much the same as they are at present, showing plainly the non-progressive nature of the Turks. It might have been thought that General Chesney's visit with his staff for the examination of the Euphrates, would have stirred the people up somewhat, but it was altogether forgotten.

We spent some time walking about the town, which was a very curious one. The side of the hill against which it was built was so steep that the floor of one house was on a level with the roof of that in front, so that the greater portion of the town was precisely like a series of steps, the tops of the houses forming one row being used as a street by those behind. The old castle, which is partly of Genoese and partly of Turkish architecture, is now a mere shell, there being only a few small rooms or huts inhabitable, which are occupied by the zaptieh and soldiers stationed in the town. Outside the town, on the south, is a level space where the caravans encamp, and where there are large open tents for the shelter of men and goods, these are the property of the government, who leases them out to men who charge for their use. In addition to these tents and the khans in the town, which are used by people travelling with mules and horses, there are also caves excavated in the soft chalk hills, which are also used as lodging-places by travellers and their animals. Some of these are very large and can accommodate a large

number of camels ; they are principally used
when the weather is too severe for people
to live under the open tents.

During our walk round the town we paid
a visit to the Kaimacan to thank him for his
civility of the previous evening, and found
him alone. Besides his raki and wine, he
now brought out some German sausage,
which, notwithstanding its being covered in
tin foil, he was at some pains to explain to
us was made of mutton in the town, lest
we should suspect him of eating the unclean
flesh of swine. Like many another Turk he
did not mind that people should know that
he did not adhere to the precepts of the
Koran respecting strong drink, but could not ·
endure to have it known that he indulged in the
unclean beast. Our noticing his gun brought
the conversation round to sport, and he said
that round Bir-ed-jik there were lots of wild
fowl, and that he often got a wild boar or a
gazelle. When we told him how the pig at
Jerablus had almost invariably taken to the

river when wounded and swum to a place
of safety, he said that when he went after
wild boar he used to take one of the ferry
boats, so that when a pig crossed the river
he was able to go after it. He asked about
our success at Jerablus in digging, but quite
scouted the idea of having sent down to
interfere with the work. He declared that
the only message he had sent, was to tell
Shaykh Hosayn to assist in every possible
way. Very likely he had really sent down
to see if we were searching for gold, as no
Turk can understand the idea of our wanting
to find out the history of the ancients. That
things have been, are, and will be, is quite
enough for them. A very curious instance
of the way the inhabitants of these countries
regard the excavations which are being made,
was brought under my own notice. A Christian family, some of the members of which
were employed in positions of trust in one
of the English parties engaged in this work,
was told by a diviner or wizard that the

English found gold when the workmen were away. This fellow declared that he could find gold for them in the same way, as he had seen some of the stones which had been dug up and was able to interpret the inscriptions. The gold he said was hidden in their house, and if they would pay him well, he promised to show it them. They paid him liberally, and acting under his instructions nearly pulled their house down in the search, and of course found nothing. Notwithstanding, they still placed full confidence in their informant, who said he had made a slight mistake, and to whom they had promised more money as soon as they were able to obtain it to go on with the search.

When we left the Kaimacan we paid a short visit to Hajji Schalbach, who welcomed us warmly and invited us to leave the khan and stay with him for a week. This of course we refused to do, and then when he had given us tea, he wished to force upon our acceptance a Russian *samovar*, in which he

had made it. He insisted that it would be
a capital thing in the tent in cold weather,
and seemed really grieved that we would not
accept it as a present. He was busy with
some carpenters belonging to the place in
constructing two carts for use in his farms,
as he had somewhere seen Circassians using
carts and had at once recognised the superiority of wheeled vehicles over pack animals.
About these he wanted our advice, but as
his carts, although very simple in their construction, seemed effective, we were not able
to be of any great use to him.

On our way back to the khan we passed a procession of small girls, trotting round the town
attired in their best, and singing and clapping
their hands. At the head was a little child of
eleven or twelve, over whose head two bigger
girls held a sort of canopy. The little girl was
covered with gold coins and other finery, and was
evidently the centre of attraction. On our asking what it was all about, we were told that
it was a *fête* in honour of her having completed

reading the *Mustafiz*, one of the Mohammedan religious books.

During the day we had had our horses shod, and replenished our stock of tobacco and provisions, so we were in fact ready to start the first thing the next morning. Our traps, indeed, were all packed up by half past six, but the muleteers wanted to make the journey to Orfa last three, instead of two days, and would not bring their mules up to be loaded without a great deal of arguing and trouble, so that it was half past ten before we started. We left in the midst of a shower of drizzling rain, first passing through numerous vineyards, and then over a hilly and broken country for about two hours; near the summits of many of the hills were numerous caves, which are used by the goatherds to shelter them and their flocks. The latter were very numerous, and amongst them were many of the goats which produce mohair.

Coming to a small building where there was a well, and which had been built as a refuge

for benighted travellers, we halted for luncheon
and to wait for our mules.   I was giving my
horse some carrots which I had bought as we
were leaving the town, when a wild looking
fellow came rushing up, and knelt down as
if to beseech assistance, but was far too excited
to say anything intelligible. Almost immediately
afterwards there appeared two men, with three
camels and a donkey.   These two had evidently
been in the wars, for one had his head bleed-
ing, and both had their clothes torn and dirty.
When they saw the kneeling man, they commenced threatening and abusing him.   After
some little time we got them composed enough
to tell their different stories, although we had
hard work to keep them from coming to
blows.   It appeared that all three had been
travelling together, the man who arrived first
having asked permission to accompany the
other two for safety and protection. About
half an hour before they met us, the two men,
who were owners of the camels, were set
upon by robbers who beat and wounded them,

and took all their money. The other man was
not molested by the robbers, and did not
attempt to assist his fellow travellers. The latter, upon this, when the robbers had departed,
took his donkey from him, and said that unless
he went with them to the town for which
they were bound, to bear witness against the
robbers, they would keep it instead of the
money of which they had been robbed. He
objected very strongly, and swore he had never
seen the robbers before, and that he was only
left alone because they saw he was too poor
to be worth robbing. We of course could
do nothing in the matter, more especially as
Mohammed, who was with us, said he thought
that most probably the donkey man was in
league with the thieves. The camel drivers
soon departed on their road, taking the donkey
with them, whilst its owner started off running
towards a hamlet some two miles away.

Our mules now came up, and the people were
all in great fright about the robbers, of whose
proximity they had been warned by some

shepherds. The most cowardly of the lot
was carrying my fowling-piece, which he had
taken out of its cover, and seemed much
astonished at being slanged for getting it wet.
The other men told us that he had proposed
to desert the baggage, and run, if the robbers
appeared whilst we were not with them, but
when he saw us he said, " Now, I will appear
brave. I will take the Captain's gun and tell
him that I was ready to defend his property
to the death," and had composed a fine set
speech to that effect, which he was very much
put out at not being able to deliver.

As we had had proof that robbers were about,
we, when we went on again, kept near to the
mules, and soon heard shouts of *Arrahmy!
Arrahmy!!* (robbers ! robbers !!) and saw
running on a course nearly parallel to the
road, about half a dozen men who seemed
to be trying to escape our observation. As
the road though now pretty level was flanked
by hills, I and the zaptieh patrolled on each
side so as to get an early view of these people

if they intended to attack us, whilst Schaefer
and Gabriel kept the mules closed up, and
placed the servants and muleteers in proper
positions to defend the baggage. After marching some miles in this warlike order, we saw
the men coming towards us with a donkey,
and they turned out to be the man whose
donkey had been taken by the camel-drivers,
and some of his friends. The owner of the
donkey now seemed quite happy, as they had
caught the camel-drivers, given them a thrash-
ing, and recovered his donkey.

The rain had been falling most of the day,
and the ground was so muddy and slippery
that we could only make very slow progress,
the loaded mules slipping and tumbling about
in a most piteous manner. At sunset we found
ourselves still far from Tsamelik, but the only
place in sight was so small and wretched that
we determined on pressing on. What with rain,
and the absence of the moon, it soon became
so dark that we could not see our horses' heads,
much less each other. The only guide to

the road was the reflection of the little light
that still lingered in the water lying in the ruts
worn by the feet of passing animals. It was a
very uncomfortable ride, wet and cold, and the
horses slipping and splashing about most dis-
agreeably. I got off, and tried to warm
myself by walking, but found the mud so heavy
and sticky, that I soon had lumps weighing
about twenty pounds on each of my boots,
whilst, notwithstanding its adhesiveness, it was
so slippery that I found great difficulty in
keeping on my feet, so that I had to get on my
horse again, and trust to his being more sure-
footed than I was.

Splash, splash, splash, on we went until at
last we came to where the track divided into
two, and no one knew which was the right one
to take ; the compass was no use, as the two
paths only differed about a couple of points in
their direction. We were nonplussed for a
time, and then we fancied we smelt smoke, so
chose the one which was nearest to the direction
we thought the smell came from. Soon the

dogs began to run, and the horses to step out more cheerfully, and then, joyful sound! we heard the barking of dogs.

'In another quarter of an hour we came to a large khan, and this was Tsamelik. The doors were closed, and we could make no one hear for some time, though we hammered at them with all our might, and shouted, and yelled. At last we heard a man inside who said that the place was closed for the night and would not be opened again for fear we were robbers; at last he opened and we went in. We found some shepherds and their flocks were the sole occupants, and from them we got about a quarter of an inch of candle; this we lit with some difficulty, and a dreary scene was before us. The goats and their owners took up all one side of the quadrangle except a small piece which, notwithstanding its being sheltered from the rain by a roof, was knee deep in mud and muck. The doors of the buildings on the other three sides were locked, so we were obliged to take shelter in this corner whilst Mohammed and one of the goatherds went to look for the man in whose charge the khan was, to get the keys. The mules came straggling in one by one, and one was so exhausted that he lay down, load and all, and Nimshi, who always took care of herself, instantly lay down on the top of him.

After another quarter of an hour Mohammed returned with the khan-keeper who opened one of the side buildings and there we found a dry stable. By this time all the mules had arrived, and we soon made ourselves comfortable, the only drawback being that we and our animals were in rather too close proximity. Supper and bed was the order of the day, and we were soon sound asleep, but were disturbed during the night by one of the horses getting loose and kicking over the box on which were placed my aneroid, thermometers and other instruments. Luckily nothing was lost or damaged, and order was soon restored.

The morning broke dull and gloomy, but as there was no halting-place between us and

Orfa, the muleteers for once bestirred themselves and we got away pretty soon.

The day's march was very nearly a repetition of the previous one, the only occurrences being, seeing some large bustards, and meeting the cadi of Diarbekr, who was on his way to the coast. The bustards we attempted to stalk, and if the mud on the road was bad, it was worse on the freshly ploughed ground where the birds were; so that after a half an hour's weary plodding after them and failing to get within rifle range, we were obliged to give up our pursuit and were glad to get on our horses again.

The cadi had an escort of half a dozen zaptieh and an officer, and was accompanied by his wives, who were carried in closely curtained *tak-tarawans* or mule litters.

The mules were so bothered by the mud that it was evening when we got to the top of the ridge of hills on the eastern side of which Orfa lies. Down the steep hill-side was cut a winding road, in some places out of the solid rock, and which had evidently required a vast amount of labour, but which was constructed on such bad principles as to be rapidly falling into a state of disrepair.

When we got into the town it was already dark, and scarcely a soul was moving about. We found our way through streets, which were knee deep in liquid mud with the exception of small raised footways, to a couple of khans, both of which the keepers declared were full. At one of these khans we got a man with a lantern who promised to show us the way to another, but who soon bolted, and we were left in pitchy darkness and not knowing where to go. We could do nothing but knock at the first door we found, and after some time the owner of the house opened it and asked what we wanted. We begged for a guide with a lantern to show us the way either to a khan where we could get lodging or else to the *serai* where we might find some official to assist us. He very kindly sent one of his servants with us to the *serai* which we found in charge of a sergeant-

major of zaptieh, all the superior officers having
gone to a party at Halil Bey's, who was one of
the notables of the town. The sergeant-major
took us into the guard-room, which was warmed
by a mangal, and gave us coffee, whilst one of his
men went for the Bimbashi. The Bimbashi
soon came from Halil Bey's and insisted on
going with us himself to find lodgings for
ourselves and animals.

He took us back to one of the khans
which had already turned us away, but which
at the voice of authority was speedily opened,
and where rooms were at once provided.
Not content with seeing us lodged, he waited
before going back to his friends to see us
comfortably established and all our wants supplied. Soon after he had gone we received
an invitation from Halil Bey to join their
party, but as we were tired, wet, and dirty
and also heard that the party would most
likely degenerate into a mere orgie towards
the small hours, we thought it best to decline
with thanks.

CHAPTER IV.

ORFA, the Edessa of the ancients, for long
played an important part in the history of the
East. Though its inhabitants were styled

barbarians by the luxurious citizens of Antioch,
the purest dialect of Syriac, the Aramœan,
was spoken in their streets and taught in
their schools and colleges.

Under the successive monarchs who assumed,
on commencing their reign, the surname of
Abgarus, its alliance was sought both by the
Romans and the Parthians, and their friend-
ship often determined the result of the wars
which were constantly being waged between
the two empires.

It was to one of these Abgari that the
famous Palladium was sent by our Saviour.
According to the tradition now related at
Orfa, the handkerchief bearing the miraculous
impression never arrived at its destination, but
in the pages of history we read of its assistance being invoked to repel the assaults of
heathen and Moslem foes.

The story told me at Orfa was that the
king Abgarus, being afflicted with leprosy, had
long sought for relief from his loathsome
disease but without effect. Hearing of a

prophet among the Jews who had healed
many of their illnesses, he sent his Prime
Minister to Jerusalem to beg for aid, and
also to offer him an asylum from the persecu-
tion of the Jews. When his envoy arrived
at Jerusalem he found our Lord teaching in
the temple, and told Him his mission. He
pleaded long and earnestly the cause of his
king and master, and our Saviour took from
him a silken handkerchief with which He
wiped His face, and returning it to the sup-
pliant said : " If your king will do likewise
his leprosy will be healed." Marvellous to
relate, on the handkerchief appeared the im-
print of our Saviour's features.

The envoy hastened back with the precious
gift, and being anxious to arrive quickly at
Orfa outstripped his escort and rode on alone.
A few miles before reaching his destination
he was attacked by robbers, and in order to
save his sacred charge from their sacrilegious
hands he cast it into a tank or reservoir
cut in the rocks.

After some time he escaped from the hands of the robbers, and naked and wounded made his way into the presence of Abgarus. When he had told his story, the king ordered his guards to accompany him to the tank, which he caused to be emptied of its contents. No handkerchief was there, but a spring of clear and sparkling water was gushing forth from the solid rock.

Abgarus, regarding this as a miracle, said that if he washed in the water it would have the same effect as if he had used the lost handkerchief. Washing he was healed and his flesh became as other men's flesh.

The spring remains to the present day and is regarded as sacred by both Christians and Mohammedans, though it seems to have lost its healing qualities, as poor lepers are always to be found there who subsist on the charities of pious visitants.

In history we find that the sacred handkerchief was long regarded as the chiefest treasure and defence of the city. After having

been lost to sight for five hundred years the
Bishop of Edessa presented it to the gaze of an
adoring multitude. It was soon credited with
having repelled the assault of Chosroes by
its presence on the ramparts, and its possession was supposed to ensure the town
from ever falling into the hands of Pagan
conquerers.

Notwithstanding the possession of this ἀχειρο-
ποίητος, and having successfully resisted her
Persian assailants, Edessa was fated to fall into
the hands of the Saracens, and the holy image
was retained by them for three hundred years,
until the piety of the rulers of Constantinople
ransomed it from their hands by payment of
twelve thousand pounds of silver, the liberation
of two hundred prisoners, and the proclama-
tion of a perpetual truce in the country around
Edessa.

Another legend which is told with all gravity,
is one about Nimrod and Abraham. Standing
out boldly above the present town, but within
the precincts of its ancient walls, are two

magnificent Corinthian columns, sole remains of
some ancient temple.   These are said to have
been erected by Nimrod "the mighty hunter
before the Lord."   He and Abraham were together at Orfa, and Abraham, presuming on his
superior piety, used to preach to Nimrod about
his evil ways and those of his followers.
Nimrod did not approve of the sermons and
determined to punish Abraham for his in-
terference.   He therefore ordered the columns
to be built, and put a swing between them.
Below he had a huge fire made, which was
so fierce that no man dared approach.   Putting
Abraham into the swing, he launched him
into the flames.   Abraham fell to the ground
in the attitude of prayer, and from the prints
made by his knees immediately gushed forth
two springs, which extinguished the flames
before they had inflicted the slightest injury on
his person or his raiment.

Over these springs, which are some forty feet
apart, is built a large mosque, and the water
flows into two large pools crowded with a

species of carp, which are daily fed by the
faithful.   The dervish who showed us the place
said that they were the soldiers of Abraham,
but one of his brethren declared that they were
the people of Nimrod—and who is to decide
when Doctors differ ?

This legend about Nimrod and Abraham
is very ancient and is referred to in the
twenty-first chapter of *Al Koran,* entitled
" The Prophets."   The reason of Nimrod per-
secuting Abraham is that the latter destroyed
the idols of Terah, his father.   The passage
itself stands as follows :—

" And this book also is a blessed admonition ; which we
have sent down from heaven : will ye therefore deny it ?
and we gave unto Abraham his direction heretofore, and we
knew him to be worthy of the revelations wherewith he was
favoured.   Remember when he said unto his father, and his
people, 'What are the images to which ye are so entirely
devoted ? '   They answered, ' We found our fathers worship-
ping them.'   He said, ' Verily both ye and your fathers have
been in manifest error.'   They said, ' Dost thou seriously
tell us the truth, or art thou one who jestest with us ? '   He
replied, ' Verily your Lord is the Lord of the heavens and
the earth ; it is He who hath created them : and I am one
of those who bear witness thereof.   By God I will surely
devise a plot against your idols, after you shall have retired
from them and shall have turned your backs.'   And in the

people's absence he went into the temple where the idols stood, and he brake them all in pieces, except the biggest of them ; that they might lay the blame upon that. And when they were returned and saw the havoc which had been made, they said, 'Who hath done this unto our gods ? He is certainly an impious person.' And certain of them answered, 'We heard a young man speak reproachfully of them : he is named Abraham.' They said, 'Bring him therefore before the eyes of the people that they may bear witness against him.' And when he was brought before the assembly, they said unto him, 'Hast thou done this unto our gods, O Abraham ?' He answered, 'Nay, that the biggest of them hath done it; but ask them, if they can speak.' And they returned unto themselves, and said the one to the other, 'Verily ye are the impious persons.' Afterwards they relapsed into their former obstinacy and said, 'Verily thou knowest that these speak not.' Abraham answered, 'Do ye therefore worship, besides God, that which cannot profit you at all, neither can he hurt you ? Fie on you, and upon that which ye worship besides God ! Do ye not understand ?' They said, 'Burn him and avenge your gods : if ye do this it will be well.' And when Abraham was cast into the pile, we said, 'O fire be thou cold and a preservation unto Abraham.' And they sought to lay a plot against him : but we caused them to be sufferers, and we delivered him and Lot by bringing them into the land where we have blessed all things."

The Jewish version on which the Mohammedan one is founded is that Abraham went into his father Terah's shop during his absence and broke the idols up. When Terah returned home he inquired how it was they had been

destroyed. Abraham replied that they had
quarrelled among themselves as to who was
to possess a beautiful flower which had been
offered to them by an old woman. Terah seeing the dilemma in which he was placed, that
if he said his gods could not fight he would
admit that they were powerless, fell into a
violent passion, and bound Abraham, and
carried him into the presence of Nimrod that
he might be punished for his sacrilegious action
and blasphemy. The Jews also translate Ur of
the Chaldees, as the fire of the Chaldees, instead of allowing that Ur is the proper name
of a city, thereby implying that Nimrod
attempted to punish Abraham by burning him.

The Mohammedan fable traverses nearly
the same ground. Abraham having concealed
himself in the temple of the heathen gods,
destroyed all the idols, save the largest, whilst
the Chaldeans were all absent at an open air
festival. Round the neck of the idol he had
spared, he hung the axe or hammer he had
used in the work of destruction. When the

Chaldeans returned, and he was questioned
about the matter, he said they could see that
Baal, as the great idol was called, had done it,
and still had the axe he had used hanging from
his neck. His countrymen were much enraged
and carried him off to Nimrod for trial, and he
was condemned to be burnt alive. According
to some this sentence was pronounced by either
a Persian Kurd, called Heyyûn, or a Magian
priest, called Andesshan, who, when he spoke
against the prophet was immediately swallowed
up alive by the earth. Others say that Nimrod
himself pronounced the sentence.

Whoever pronounced Abraham's doom it
was Nimrod who attempted to carry it into
execution. He ordered a large place at Cûtha
to be inclosed and filled with a vast quantity
of firewood. When the pile was fired it burnt
so fiercely that none durst approach it. Nimrod
ordered Abraham to be bound, and then
placing him in an engine, specially provided by
the devil, shot him into the midst of the
fire. The angel Gabriel came to Abraham's

assistance, so that the fire did him no harm, and only burnt the cords which confined him. It is added that the fire having miraculously lost its power over Abraham, became to him as a pleasant and odoriferous air, whilst two thousand of the idolaters were consumed by it.

Nimrod on seeing this miraculous deliverance cried out that he would make a sacrifice to the God of Abraham, and offered four thousand cattle. He soon, however, relapsed into his former infidelity, and after failing to reach heaven by means of the tower of Babel again renewed the attempt by means of four enormous birds, who carried a chest in which he had placed himself. This also failed, and finding his efforts against God could not prevail, he again turned his attention to Abraham. Abraham called to his assistance vast swarms of gnats, one of which penetrated into Nimrod's ear, and caused him such horrible pain that he caused his head to be beaten with a mallet in order to relieve it. This torture he endured until his death which occurred four hundred years afterwards.

These fables are not only believed by many Jews and Mohammedans, but also by a large proportion of the Eastern Christians. In the Syrian Church, the twenty-fifth of January (the second *Canûn*) is celebrated as the anniversary of Abraham being delivered from the flames, and the second of July (*Thamûz*) as that of the death of Nimrod.

The position of Edessa at the foot of the mountains and on the borders of the great Mesopotamian plain rendered it a position of great strategical importance, and Sapor I., by its acquisition, was enabled to extend his ravages even to Antioch and Homs; whilst on his retreat, when harassed by Odenathus of Palmyra, husband of the famous Zenobia, he was obliged to purchase the neutrality of the inhabitants by giving to them all the plunder he had carried off from the temple of Venus at Homs.

Constantius made it his head-quarters when threatened by Sapor II. in the East, and the

rebellion of his cousin Julian in the West.
After his death, and Julian had assumed the
imperial purple, the Christians of the town were
unlucky enough to draw upon themselves the
anger of the latter monarch, who despoiled them
of all their goods, and aggravated his tyranny
by the following biting and ironical speech :—

"I show myself the true friend of the
Galileans. Their *admirable* law has promised
the kingdom of Heaven to the poor ; and they
will advance with more diligence in the paths
of virtue and salvation when they are relieved
by my assistance from the load of temporal
possessions."

In the wars between Chosroes and Justinian,
we again find Edessa occupying a most important place, and it was mainly owing to the
repulse of Chosroes by its gallant garrison that
he agreed to a truce of five years. It was
during this siege that the Palladium was alleged
to have aided in repulsing the assailants, and
by its presence on the walls to have contributed
to the destruction of their engines by fire.

Fifty years later the mutinous conduct of the Roman army, which shook the empire to its foundations, reached its culminating point at Edessa, where the soldiers overturned the statues of the emperors, and cast stones at the miraculous handkerchief, and were only induced to return to their allegiance by large gifts from the Emperor Maurice.

Submerged by the wave of Saracen conquest, Edessa was won back to the rule of the cross by Baldwin, younger brother of Godfrey de Bouillon first king of Jerusalem. Though wearing the garments of a crusader and bound by their oaths, he did not scruple to act treacherously to a Christian in order to enrich himself. Edessa at that time, though subject to the Moslems, was a Christian town and ruled by an Armenian. This Armenian asked Baldwin, to deliver him and his people from the yoke of the Saracens. Baldwin accepted the invitation, and calling himself the son and champion of the unfortunate ruler was admitted into the town. Murdering his host and possessing himself of his treasure, he established himself in power, and founded a Christian principality in Mesopotamia, which lasted for over half a century. To this county of Edessa, the family of Courtenay afterwards became heirs, and the only surviving branch of the family are the Courtenays of England, in whose line for some time has been the Earldom of Devon, and who for more than six hundred years have filled a worthy place in English history, notwithstanding their regretful motto, " *Ubi lapsus, quid feci.*"

Towards the end of the first half of the twelfth century the Turkish hero Zenghi, after a siege of twenty five days, stormed the city of Edessa, and though he lost his life he subjected her again to Mohammedan domination under which she still labours.

A city with such a varied and momentous history cannot be supposed to boast of many remains, and the two columns are the most important; a few square minarets mark the spots where a Christian church has been degraded into a Mohammedan mosque, and the walls and other traces of fortifications are still in a fair state of preservation.

Early in the morning we received a visit from the Bimbashi, who came down to see that we were treated with all due respect and comfortably lodged. We invited him to come to dinner with us, and ordered Elias to show what skill he possessed in order to do honour to the occasion. The Bimbashi rode down on a very handsome horse, and when we admired it he asked us to pay a visit to his stables where he said he had ten horses and mares all of good breed. Soon after, he left Monsieur Martin the French Vice-Consul, to whom we had a letter of introduction from his father-in-law, Mr. Nahoun (dragoman to the English Consulate at Aleppo), and up-braided us very much for not having come to his house the night before instead of going to a khan. He wished us to change our quarters at once, but we had made our room so comfortable that we were loth to sacrifice our

independence. We could not invite him to
dinner to meet the Bimbashi, owing to our
stock of spoons, forks, etc., being too limited,
but made him promise to come on the morrow
to have luncheon with us. He quite wondered
at the way we had arranged our room. A
mere cell of a room, with a door and window
and rough stone walls, we had converted into
a comfortable-looking apartment. Round the
walls we had put the sides of our tent and
eked them out by plaids. Our trunks covered
with plaids and rugs formed seats, and our
table covered with books and writing materials
was in the middle. Guns were ranged in order,
and on some large nails which we always
carried for the purpose were hung our pistols,
belts, field glasses, and compasses. Aneroids,
thermometers, and watches were arranged on
their board, and it looked quite as if we had
taken a permanent lease of the place instead
of being mere wayfaring wanderers.

When Monsieur Martin left, another visitor
came dressed in European clothes, and wearing

a fez, who instantly commenced with "How is your health; I hope the country is pleasant as you find it." This gave me hopes that we were to be able to have a conversation in English, but though our friend informed us that he was the master of an English school, and rolled out his first questions easily enough, he could not keep up a fluent conversation. He had great complaints to make about the way in which the Christians were treated, but was very vague in what he said. I asked him to tell me any instances of ill-usage or hardship so that I might write to our consul on the subject, but he would only say, "In every way."

"It is no use telling us that they are badly used in every way; let us know some particular case and we will write about it."

"Oh! they are treated like slaves."

"But how? Slaves are sometimes treated very well."

"Oh! we are badly used in every way that slaves can be badly used."

I of course had to tell him again that a general and vague complaint was of little or no use, but that any well authenticated case of ill-usage or hardship I would report at once. All we could get out of him was that the Christians were despised by the Mohammedans and looked upon as an inferior race. When he left we went and called on the Pasha, who was just on the point of starting for Aleppo, and his *locum tenens*, a friend and country-man of Khamil Pasha, was with him. The Pasha talked cleverly, as many Turks do, about the necessity of roads and railways ; but as we heard his presence at Aleppo was required to answer a charge of malappro-priation of public funds, I suppose he was no better than any other of the Pashas who are supposed to govern Asiatic Turkey.

As we left the Pasha's rooms we came upon our portly friend the Bimbashi and the Sergeant-Major. With the former we had coffee, and whilst in his room made the acquaintance of a dervish, who spoke a little French and promised

to show us the holes made by the knees of
Abraham. After this we called on Monsieur
Martin and made the acquaintance of his wife
and children. Monsieur Martin has bought
'a' large tract of country near Orfa, which he
cultivates, and exports the wheat. Notwithstanding his title deeds having been made out
and legalised at Constantinople, he was not
allowed by successive governors to enter upon
full possession until he had paid heavy bribes ;
three or four times he gave fifty pounds, but
though allowed to cultivate his land they would
not register his deeds. At last he was tired
of frittering away his money, and paid two
hundred and fifty pounds in one sum which
had the desired effect. He said he was very
successful but the scarcity and cost of carriage
weighed heavily on him. In good seasons he
told us that he often sent off twelve hundred
camels in one day.

He was full of information and stories, and
told me the legends about Abgarus and Nimrod,
and also one about Tsamelik. Three small

kings seeing that there was no shelter for
travellers on the road between Bir-ed-jik and
Orfa, built the khan where we had slept.
Other kings, whose names are forgotten, hearing they were building a fortress sent an army
against them and killed them. The names
of the jealous monarchs are lost but Tsamelik
preserves the memory of the three who built
the khan.

He had spent much time among the Bedouins,
and told us some stories about their generosity
and sense of honour and hospitality. " Once
an Arab Shaykh possessed a mare which was
reputed to be the best in the whole region, and
though many a stratagem and wile had been
employed by his enemies and rivals to obtain
possession of her, none had succeeded. At
last, one day as he was approaching a spring
where he was going to rest, he saw a poor
beggar apparently unable to walk lying by the
wayside. He dismounted and placed the
sufferer on his mare. The moment the latter
was mounted he started off, and said, " Son

of such a one, I am so and so, and I have obtained possession of your mare."

The owner said, "So be it, but promise me two things—the first that you will treat the mare well, the second that you will never tell any one how you obtained her, as it will prevent people from assisting the poor and needy." The robber was so struck by his generosity, that he dismounted from the mare and returned her to her owner, and the two were ever after fast friends.

Another story was about the conduct of an Arab towards a European. The latter had been visiting a Shaykh, and on leaving left behind him a knife. This was found and brought to the Shaykh; he did not know where his guest was gone, and therefore could not return it to him. Some fifteen or twenty years after, the two met once more, and the Shaykh, showing him camels, sheep, and horses, said, "Those are your property." His friend was astonished, and asked how this could be. "Do you not remember leaving a knife behind you

when you were with me before? I could not
send it to you, and I could not keep it to be
eaten by rust, so I sold it for a she camel;
from that camel and her produce, and by
trading, I have amassed these animals, and
now they are yours."

Our dinner in the evening to the Bimbashi
was a great success. The next day we visited
the mosque of Abraham, fed the fishes, inspected the horses of the Bimbashi and rode
two of them, and in the evening dined with
the Martins.

Next morning Schaefer and I started with
Daher and Elias, leaving Gabriel in charge
of the other servants and dogs and of our
baggage under Monsieur Martin's roof, for
Diarbekr, where we had promised to go to
visit Major Trotter. As usual engaging fresh
mules was a great deal of trouble, and if it
had not been for the Bimbashi's aid we should
not have got away when we did. Even with
his assistance the four that we did get were
wretched tired brutes, and it was past ten

o'clock before we started in the midst of
pelting rain.

The Bimbashi had given us besides our old
zaptieh another, Ibrahim Chaoush, as he said
the Kurds, through whose country we would
be travelling, were in a very unsettled state,
and that it was better for us to be a strong
party. The rain continued to fall, and the
mud was deep often up to the horses' houghs,
in other places it was so slippery that they
could hardly stand. About three F.M., as we
were passing through a village, we were stopped
by a venerable old man who brought out coffee
and wanted us to stop for the night, but we
were determined to make the best of our way
and pressed on. This old man we found was
the father of Ibrahim Chaoush and he utterly
refused a small tip which we offered him. At
about half an hour after sunset we reached a
village in which amidst squalid huts stood a
very nice-looking stone house. This was the
habitation of the head man, who instantly put
his reception room at our disposal. At one end

was a large fireplace with a chimney and a cheerful fire of brushwood and camels' dung blazing merrily. This we were not sorry to see and to avail ourselves of it to dry our soaking clothes and boots.

The old gentleman to whom the house belonged and some of his sons and friends bore us company and joined in our meal, and in tea-drinking afterwards. The tea they seemed to relish on account of the sugar, and much amusement was caused by one of the sons being found with five large lumps in his hand when he was asking for more.

The father was a very rich man, owning flocks and herds and a very large number of Angora goats. He had been a traveller in his day, having visited Cairo and Constantinople, and still had correspondents in Aleppo to whom he consigned his wool.

Next morning there was scarcely any improvement in the weather or the road, though some of the streams were bridged ; but often the pitch of the bridge was so steep and the

roadway so bad that it was much safer to ford
the stream. No camels were to be seen on
the road, as it was too dangerous for them to
travel; but we constantly met mules bearing
huge loads of hides, wool, and other produce
of Kurdistan. We also passed caravans, composed entirely of donkeys, and as they were
very diminutive, and their packs very big, so
that one could only see legs and head, the sight
was peculiar. Though apparently overloaded,
the little beasts seemed to get along merrily.
The rain in the afternoon was almost con-
tinuous, and the badness of the road such that
we could not move out of a walk, and that of
the slowest description; so that when it fell
dark we were still three hours away from
Severik, the half-way point between Orfa and
Diarbekr. Under these circumstances we were
glad to avail ourselves of the shelter afforded
us by a Kurdish village. We had to grope
our way into a dark room, off which branched
other places in which were herded cattle, goats,

sheep, dogs and human beings, in promiscuous confusion. We got one of these dens—it deserved no better name—cleared of its motley occupants and the thick of the dirt shovelled out—much to the astonishment of the Kurds, who could not understand why we were so "nasty particular,"—and ensconced ourselves in it. The roof was leaky, huge black drops of soot and water kept falling on us, and the fire we had was of green or damp wood, and emitted a most sharp and penetrating smoke, causing our eyes to smart and well-nigh choking us by its acrid fumes.

Luckily we had brought with us the large waterproof ground sheet of our tent, and with that we managed to rig up a sort of shelter, under which we ate and slept.

We were delighted next morning to find that the rain had ceased and the clouds cleared away ; nor were we long in making our start. Mules and men, however, were so tired that we only went as far as Severik, and telegraphed on to Major Trotter that we should be a day late in arriving at Diarbekr.

We found a very good khan and a good Turkish bath close by, and both were acceptable after our experiences of the night before.

CHAPTER V.

COMING back from the Turkish bath to the khan
we found as usual a bevy of visitors. The first
to address us was a man who might have been
twin brother of the English teacher at Orfa, who
used the same form of " How is your health ? "
and who rambled on in the same way about
the oppressions and hardships under which the

Christians laboured. After much pressing and cross-examination we found out two grievances which he considered tangible : one was that a Christian and a Mohammedan having fought, both had been punished : and the other was that though they had permission from Constantinople to build a Protestant Church, the local government had only given them a site, and had refused to contribute anything to the cost of the edifice.

In addition to this gentleman we were honoured by the presence of the Syrian Bishop and some of his clergy, who were more contained in their complaints, but who evidently were not, even after long centuries of oppression, bearing the Turkish yoke with comfort. The Armenian Bishop sent a messenger to excuse himself from calling on us, as he was too fat to leave his house.

When our visitors left we wandered about the town, which was full of travellers, being a point where many tracks crossed, and which was anciently no doubt of great importance.

The citadel, or rather its remains, was, as usual in comparatively plain countries, an artificial hill cased with masonry, and though not so large or imposing as that of Aleppo, it was still of considerable size. The name of the town most probably is derived from Severus, as the troops both of Severus Septimius and Alexander Severus must have passed by this place in their campaigns against the Parthians and Persians.

The bazaars were much the same as those in all small towns, and we bought woollen gloves and stockings for our men, as between Severik and Diarbekr the snow was reported to be lying in great quantities, and the cold to be very severe. Circassians were present in great numbers, who were intending to join their compatriots who had been planted in the country round Diarbekr after the Crimean war, and were waiting for more temperate weather before resuming their journey. Here, instead of being paid in money for their subsistence, they were given corn out of the public granaries, and the

scene of confusion at the place where it was
served out was great indeed. The Circassians,
being much more numerous than the people
appointed to give them their allowance, broke
in upon the heaps of grain, and carried off as
much as they could, besides wasting more.

When we returned again to the khan a man
came to us, who said he had been chief musician
to Daoud Pasha when he was governor of the
Lebanon ; and he asked if he and his companions
might come and play before us in the evening.
We agreed, and accordingly after supper they
came into our room. The chief man had a
sort of guitar with a very long handle, and
the only idea he had of playing it was running
a piece of iron like a knitting-needle across
the strings. He was accompanied by two other
instrumentalists, and two boys who were to
dance. The other instruments were a harp
and a fiddle : the first on a sort of sounding-
board, which was laid flat on the ground while
the player twanged the strings with iron tips
on his forefingers. The fiddle had three strings,

and a very small round body with long projections, to the ends of which the strings were attached, so that the bridge was nearly in the centre of them. The bow which the fiddler used had the hair quite slack, and was tightened by the way in which it was grasped. The performance commenced with music and singing. The principal vocalist was the guitar-player, who, if he was not much as a singer, contorted his face to an extent that almost repaid us for the discordant sounds he emitted from his mouth by the extraordinary grimaces he made. His mouth opened and shut like a rusty rat-trap, and the jagged appearance of his teeth heightened the resemblance. The dancing followed afterwards, the two boys being dressed up in petticoats, and having bells attached to their feet and hands. This does not bear description; indeed we bundled the whole party out of the room before it had gone on two minutes, much to their astonishment and surprise. Daoud Pasha's bandmaster complained of his treatment at our hands, and said he was only giving an entertainment which he was always asked for by the Turks. We paid him for his music, and told him if he ever dared to come near us again we would smash his guitar over his head.

Once our room was clear, an admiring audience having stolen in at one end, we went to bed intending to make an early start in the morning, and slept more comfortably than we had done the night before in the Kurdish hovel. ·

At half-past five in the morning we were awake, and on the road by half-past six.

A made road had commenced a short distance before we arrived at Severik and up to the town had been fairly good; and indeed with very little trouble might have been made quite fit for wheeled carriages. This we were told went all the way to Diarbekr, and we flattered ourselves we should be able to travel quickly and easily. Soon after quitting the town we found that the road was worse than where nothing had been attempted; great lumps of

basalt had been piled together in some places
to form a foundation and nothing more had
been done.   It had frozen hard during the
night, and a bitter cold north-east wind was
blowing from over the snow-clad mountains,
but the sun was shining strongly, so that the
surface of the ground was half thawed and
so slippery that the animals could scarcely get
along.   Getting down to walk was hopeless,
as it was almost impossible to keep our feet,
and the lumps of stone, small rocks, with
which the ground was. strewn, made it very
difficult for one to move at all.   Luckily
our horses were surer footed than we were,
and they did manage to crawl along.   At
3,500 feet above the sea we came upon large
drifts' of snow lying in places where they were
sheltered from the sun, and in front we could
see that the Karaja Dagh was completely
covered.

After seven hours of floundering along, we
came to a small Kurdish village, and were
able to get on the lee side of a hut and in

the full sun to give our horses a rest and get luncheon for ourselves. The sun was so powerful that, although in the wind it was painfully cold, sheltered from the north-east gale we got quite warm and comfortable.

We got barley for our horses from the Kurds, and when they had eaten it, started again along a rather better piece of road, and where we were both somewhat sheltered from the wind and also enjoyed the rays of the sun.

Very few wayfarers were seen,—a few peasants with small loads packed on the backs of diminutive bullocks or still more diminutive asses, a party of zaptieh, and a band of sturdy beggars wearing green turbans. These last claimed charity as a right, alleging that they were descendants of the prophet, and when refused hurled curses and imprecations at our heads, and would no doubt have resorted to more forcible arguments if they had not been deterred by our arms.

Just before sunset we arrived at the village

of Kara-Bagh-shu. From the road scarce a
sign of human habitation was visible, except
the wreaths of smoke curling in the air, the
exterior walls of the houses being only four
or five feet high, and composed of loose
rough stones, often sloping, and the flat roofs
having, if anything, more vegetation on them
than the stony ground around, on which
goats and cows were grazing. Here we
found shelter for the night in one of the
houses, all the people having rooms for the
accommodation of travellers and their animals;
as all people passing between Severik and
Diarbekr break their journey at Kara-Bagh-
shu. The interiors of the houses were perfectly dark, the walls innocent of any attempt
at plastering, and the floors were rough earth
interspersed with huge stones.

Into one of these dens we packed ourselves
and followers, whilst our animals occupied
another. If all inside was dark, squalid, and
ugly, the scenery outside was lovely, and the
rays of the setting sun reflected from the

snow-clad mountains beautiful in the extreme; range upon range of mountains of every shape and form, glistening like gems and changing their colour every moment, with a dark foreground and backed by a sky which close to the horizon was of the deepest crimson, and by insensible gradations changed into pure deep blue at the zenith.

We stopped looking at the gorgeous sight until the last colours faded from view and the stars shone out bright and clear, and were not sorry to find a blazing fire burning in our lodging place, and that Elias had a hot supper ready for us.

We had at Severik received a telegram from Major Trotter, asking us by which road we intended to arrive, as he would come out to meet us; this we had not been able to answer definitely, as none of our people had any idea as to which was the best. We now called into our aid the experience of our host, and he said that there were two ways—one by following the line of the apology for a road, which we had been on since leaving Severik, and the other by striking straight across the crest of the Karaja-Dagh. The latter was much the shortest, but the road was bad and there was much snow, though as we had no heavily laden animals it would be quite easy for us to pass it; and we should gain so much time that most probably we should be able to reach Diarbekr before any one coming to meet us would have started, and that for a small payment he would put us into the right way.

We accordingly agreed with him, and by sunrise next morning were on our way. Kara-Bagh-shu was four thousand four hundred feet above the sea, and snow in patches lay nearly a thousand feet lower down, but we had to climb a steep and rocky path for nearly five hundred feet until we came into an unbroken sheet of white. Across this snow we should have been unable to pass without the local knowledge of our guide, as all minor inequalities were smoothed over and hidden by its treacherous mantle. Indeed, even with him to show us the way, we often got into snow so deep that we had to retrace our steps and try another line. On the snow were the tracks numberless of hares, and partridges, and also of wild pig. In one place which seemed open, we saw a party of seven pig crossing the snow with apparent ease, and making for the shelter of a wood of dwarf oaks. Such an opportunity was not to be lost, so unslinging my rifle I started Sultan after them; but we had not got twenty yards before we landed in such a depth of snow that further progress became impossible. The snow was nearly up to his withers, and it was with great difficuly we extricated ourselves. I had to dismount, and roll on the snow, so as to make room for the horse to turn round and get back; of course by the time we were clear, the pig were out of sight.

Just beyond this place we crossed the crest of the mountain, which I made six thousand two hundred and fifty feet above the sea, and on the other side of what to us seemed a wide plain

we could see the walls and towers of Diarbekr.
Here our guide left us, and we made the
descent, if not without many a slip and slide,
still without any accident, owing to the marvellous sure-footedness of our horses. As we
left the snow we found crocuses of varied
colours growing at its very edge, in some
instances the flowers even appeared actually
in the midst of snow. As we descended it got
warmer and warmer, and when we were at the
foot of the mountains the temperature was very
pleasant. As the time we had taken crossing
the mountains had considerably exceeded what
we had expected, we now put our horses into
a canter and made the best of our way.

Although from the mountain top Diarbekr
had seemed almost at our feet and the plain
smooth and unbroken, we now found the town
still distant, and the plain broken by deep
valleys at the bottom of which ran streams
flowing to the Tigris. The country was
cultivated in many places, but not to a quarter
or a fifth of the extent of which it is capable.

As we drew near the town we saw a man riding towards us who turned out to be one of Major Trotter's servants, and who said that his master and some of his friends had gone out to meet us by the other road, and galloped off to tell them. We were asked to sit down on a carpet, which was brought out from a neighbouring house, and await their return. We soon saw them coming back, and besides Major Trotter, there was an Englishman—agent for the Constantinople firm who supply Messrs. Salt, of Saltair, with mohair—the French vice-consul, Mr. Pisani in charge of telegraphs, and some others. We rode into the town in quite an imposing form ; and Major Trotter put us up most comfortably at his house.

Major Trotter's presence at Diarbekr at this time was partly owing to the Kurdish insurrection at Jezireh which is in the vilayet of Diarbekr. He had been all through the war, on Sir Arnold Kemball's staff, and was appointed consul for Erzeroum on account of his intimate knowledge of the country, and from Erzeroum had been ordered to Diarbekr on the outbreak of the Kurdish troubles.

Stories were flying about in all directions about this insurrection, but many were exaggerated, and all showed the extraordinary manner in which the country is administered, and supposed to be governed. By the Sultans Mahmoud II. and Abdul Medjid the power of the great hereditary chiefs of the Kurds was broken, and the feudal system abolished. Before these changes, each chief ruled supreme in his own district, and only gave aid to the Sultan in time of war, when they were bound to take the field with their followers against the enemy. Of course quarrels and fights were rife among the various sections of the Kurds, and the unfortunate Nestorian Christians who lived near them were plundered and ill-used by all.

When the old system was done away with, the children of the principal beys and aghas were sent to various towns to be educated far away from their own people and home associations. The two brothers, Bahri Bey and Osman Bey, were sons of the chief among all the beys, and were sent, with other of their brothers, to be educated at Damascus. Some of the family were taken into the Sultan's service, and one brother is cupbearer to the Sultan, and another one of his aïdes-de-camp. The latter was placed on the staff of Izzet Pasha—the general who was given command of the expedition sent to quell the insurrection.

As the story of the insurrection was told to me it was not destitute of grim humour; and traces of loyalty to their hereditary chiefs were shown by the descendants of their fathers. These beys when in their own country are called mirs or princes, and the greatest oath their adherents can take is "by the head of their mir." When these call upon the people, all other ties and duties are forgotten, whether to God, to the Sultan, or to their families. The present Sultan is said to be closely related to this family; and the following celebrated persons— Saladdin, the chivalrous enemy of Richard Cœur de Lion, the Lady Zobeide, wife of the

Caliph Haroun-al-Raschid, Zenghi, the captor
of Edessa, and his son Noureddin, at once the
most powerful and most humble of the servants
of the Abassides—are claimed by its members
as being amongst the number of their ancestors.

Bahri Bey and Osman Bey, according to
their own account, being weary of inaction, and
having in vain solicited the Sultan for em-
ployment against the Muscovites, determined
to do something to show that they were still
men and not unworthy of their mighty an-
cestry. Nothing seemed more suitable than
that they should proceed to their native country
and there resume the property of which, in
their opinion, their father had been unjustly
deprived.

With this object they came to Kurdistan,
and assuming the national dress, issued pro-
clamations to the adherents of their family.
They soon found themselves at the head of
about four thousand armed men, and, marching
upon Jezireh, made themselves masters of that

place. When they arrived the Kaimacan asked them by what authority they seized upon the reins of government, to which they replied that they had private letters from the Sultan authorising them in their course of action. When they took charge of the treasury and telegraph office and ordered the Turkish troops to obey them instead of the Kaimacan, he said he must insist upon seeing their instructions. They replied they would show him them immediately, and sent for him into a room which was almost full of their followers. "You want our instructions? Very well, we will give them you," said they; and then, ordering a sheep to be killed, they took off the Kaimacan's fez and replaced it by the intestines of the sheep, saying, "There are our instruc· tions." With this upon his head, the poor Kaimacan was forced to dance by men menacing and pricking him with their swords, whilst the Beys and their intimate. friends clapped their hands and jeeringly complimented him on his grace and activity.

Having seized on the telegraph office, they amused themselves by sending most absurd messages to the governors of Diarbekr and Mosul, telling them to attend at the offices in those places, that they might give them orders and directions, and saying that they would shortly come to carry out the Sultan's orders in their towns as well as at Jezireh. From many of the inhabitants of Jezireh they extorted forced loans; and one unfortunate Christian, after the whole thing was over, was condemned to two years' imprisonment for having lent money to armed rebels.

For a time all seemed to go well with the brothers, but some of the other Kurdish chiefs looked upon the insurrection with disfavour, as being likely to diminish their power and authority, and refused their adherence.

Bahri Bey and Osman Bey marched against one of these, an agha, who possessed a sort of castle on the top of a high hill, taking with them about four thousand Kurds and the Turkish garrison of Jezireh which numbered about a hundred. The agha could only oppose eighteen hundred men to their forces, but favoured by his position he successfully defended himself for some time, and at last the tide of battle was turned in his favour by the Turkish troops joining his side. The adherents of the brothers fled pell-mell into Jezireh, whither they were pursued by their foes, who restored the Kaimacan to his place and authority. News of the termination of the rebellion was at once telegraphed, but it did not avail to stop the march of Izzet and his troops. Abdul-Rahman, the wali of Diarbekr, at once proceeded to Jezireh to restore order, but was very much hurt by the Sultan ignoring both his ministers at Constantinople and his officers in the provinces, by telegraphing direct to the insurgents. He said, "We want reforms, but they should begin at the head." The terms of the telegram were that if the two Beys would submit and come to Constantinople, they would receive great honours, pensions, and rewards.

We saw them afterwards arrive in Diarbekr escorted by cavalry, and by infantry, mounted on mules; riding with their brother, the aide-de-camp, and having more the appearance of honoured guests than captive rebels. Both the Beys were fine-looking, handsome men, and were dressed in the very extreme of Kurdish dandyism. Conical felt caps nearly three feet high, with coils of gaudy silk handkerchiefs reaching about half way up; a close-fitting bearskin jacket without sleeves and open in front; gaudy waistcoats with gold and silver buttons, open hanging sleeves of striped silk sweeping the ground, and tight under sleeves also of silk; an enormous sash stuck full of pistols and daggers, trousers, loose and baggy, of striped silk, and bright-coloured morocco shoes very much turned up at the toes, completed their costume, which certainly in its wild and barbaric style was a very striking and handsome one.

In their train were several *taktarawans*, or horse litters, containing women and children all gaudily arrayed. These they had collected in the country, and were taking to Constantinople with them to pass off as their wives and children, and so appeal both to the head and heart of the Sultan ;—to his head by proving that as married men and fathers of families they might be trusted not to provoke causeless disturbances, and to his heart by showing how many widows and orphans they would leave if anything were to happen to them.

So far however from its being necessary to appeal to the Sultan for pity, he seemed to have been only too well inclined towards them, for it was currently reported at Diarbekr that he had conferred the first class of the Osmanlie. on one of them, and this rumour I have since seen confirmed in some of the English papers.

To reward rebels and punish the innocent seems to be one of the ideas of the Turkish Government, and that it has borne fruit may be seen by the new Kurdish revolt, which has

not even yet come to an end. The Sultan's
paltering with these chiefs I have seen termed
a judicious mixture of moderation and force;
I call it a premium on revolt, and an incitement
to disloyalty.

CHAPTER VI.

DIARBEKR is the ancient Amida, and by the
Turks is called Kara Amid or Black Amid,
to the present day. The name of Diarbekr
is of Arab origin, and means the country of
Bekr. It is called 'Black Amid from the black
basalt of which the greater portion of the city
is built. Inhabitants of other towns say that

at Kara Amid, the stones are black, the dogs
are black, and the hearts of the people are
black.   Curiously enough the prevailing colour
of the pariah dogs, which act as scavengers in
the streets, is black, instead of the usual dirty
dun yellow.

Amida is mentioned in the Assyrian records,
and was the royal city destroyed by Asshur-
·izi-pal in his tenth campaign ; this was
between 860 and 870 B.C.   It opposed a
valiant resistance to Sapor II.   After he had
defeated the Roman armies in the open field,
Sapor, in the pride of conquest, thought that
his mere appearance before the walls would be
sufficient to awe the garrison and inhabitants
into surrendering.   A shower of darts—one of
which penetrated his armour, though without
wounding him—convinced him of his error.
He then ordered Grumbates, king of the
Chionites to take the town by assault, but this
failed likewise, Grumbates' only son being killed
by his side.   The endeavours of the besiegers
did not relax on account of this repulse, but

they adopted the more patient means of sap
and mine, and regularly invested the place.
The besieged still held out with unabated
courage, though the reliefs under Sabinianus
which they had a right to expect, did not
appear, and notwithstanding the treachery of
one of the inhabitants who introduced a part
of the Persian guard into one of the bastions,
it was not until the seventy-third day that the
Persians made their way into the town. The
time Amida had resisted had saved the Syrian
provinces of the Roman empire, and Sapor
gratified his rage by slaying many of the gallant
garrison in cold blood, and crucifying the noble
Romans who had conducted the defence.

Amida soon rose again from her ruins, and
was usually regarded as the capital of the
kingdom of Armenia; she received within her
walls the inhabitants of Nisibin when Jovian,
the unworthy and pusillanimous successor of
Julian, drove them from their homes in obedience to the demands of the Persians. The
misfortunes of others proved in this case the

good fortune of Amida, for this influx of worthy
citizens aided her in establishing and maintain-
ing her pre-eminence amongst the cities of
Armenia ; but later in her history she was
again doomed to be besieged and taken by the
Persians under Kobad or Cobades.   Huns and
Arabs alike marched under the standards of
the Persian monarch.   Although Amida was
only defended by a small force under Alypius,
the monks inspired the inhabitants to make
a vigorous resistance.   The walls were strong,
and resisted the engines of the Persians, and
a huge mound erected by them to dominate
the fortifications was undermined and ruined
by the besieged.   Three months elapsed, and
thirty thousand of the besiegers perished
without any impression being made on the
town.   Kobad was inclined to discontinue the
siege, but the prophecies of the magi, who said
that the indecent insults of the women of the
town were sure omens of success of the Persian
arms, decided him to persevere.

At length an entrance to one of the towers,

which was imperfectly built up, was discovered, by which a party of Persian troops were able to make an entrance. The garrison of the tower consisted of monks who were sleeping off the effects of a debauch in which they had indulged on account of a festival, and were easily surprised. The Persian army poured into the town, and commenced an indiscriminate massacre. An aged priest had the courage to remonstrate with the victorious monarch, and to tell him it was unworthy of a king to slaughter captives.

Kobad asked why they elected to fight, to which the priest replied, "It was God's doing. He willed that thou shouldst owe the conquest of Amida not to our weakness, but to thine own valour."

This timely flattery availed to stop the slaughter, but the town was sacked and the inhabitants carried off into slavery.

In 504 Patricius and Hypatius laid siege to the Persian garrison of Amida, and it was on the point of surrendering when an ambassador

arrived from the Persian monarch offering to
restore all his conquests on the payment of a
thousand pounds' weight of gold. Ignorant
of their opponent's difficulties and of the
condition of the garrison, they agreed to the
terms, and Amida again passed into their
hands.

The very walls of Diarbekr tell the history of
its varying fortunes.   Though still very perfect,
indeed more so than those of any other town
we visited, they bear evident signs of having
been rebuilt many times.   Stones with Greek
and Cufic inscriptions are built into the walls
in vague confusion, in many places the writing
being upside down, and on some may be
seen rude sculptures much resembling the
hieroglyphics on the sculptures we found at
Karchemish.   The citadel was on an artificial
mound, and inclosed in an inner circle of walls,
whilst in ancient days the Tigris swept by in
the bottom of the valley, close to the artificially
formed cliff on which the outer wall rested.   The
soil of the valley of the Tigris is here formed

by a flat mass of alluvium, and the river varies
its course constantly, so that some day again
it may run close to the base of the walls as
described by ancient writers.

A short distance below the town is the bridge
of Diarbekr, which spans the Tigris where the
two sides of the valley approach each other.
This bridge bears marks of vicissitudes similar
to those which have happened to the walls,
though in all probability the centre was never
destroyed, as it is wider there than, at the sides,
and the arches are formed of Roman bricks,
and are of a greater span than those close
to the banks, which are neither so bold nor
so well constructed. Some Cufic inscriptions
are on this bridge, and the mason's marks
on the stones may still be seen on the lower
part of the piers. The importance of this
bridge is considered to be so great, that when
an Arab chief was about to pull down the walls
of the town in fulfilment of a vow he had made
to destroy its importance, his sister persuaded
him to demolish the bridge instead, as it was

to it, and not to her walls, that Diarbekr owed
her prosperity.   The bridge, however, still
remains, and leading from it on the right bank
of the river is a road which was constructed
some thirty years ago by Ismail Pasha, and
which is called Ismail's railway by the country
people.

Inside the walls of the town are numerous
remains of great interest, the most important
being that of a heathen temple.   At each
end of a large paved quadrangle are rows of
columns and above these a second row.   These
columns are of different sorts of stone and
of different patterns.   In the centre of the
quadrangle is a fountain, and along one side
is a large mosque of no architectural pre-
tensions.   The present level of the courtyard
is much higher than it was in ancient days,
and no doubt if search could be made many
interesting Roman remains might be found.
Christianity established itself at a very early
date in Diarbekr, and one church is said to
date from the end of the first century of the

Christian era. It consists of a building with two domes, one of which was over the sanctuary and the part where those who were baptised used to worship, whilst the other sheltered the place devoted to the catechumens. The first dome was still perfect and under it were a large quantity of Peabody rifles; these, which had been bought in America and transported here at an enormous cost, were utterly neglected, and in such a state of rust and decay that most probably more than half of them were entirely useless. In the space under the other dome, the top of which had fallen into disrepair, were piled Enfield and Minie rifles, and cavalry lances like sticks in a faggot pile. Near this church was the wreck of a building which was reported to have been the palace of one of the Armenian kings, and which, till a few years ago, had been quite perfect; but being used as a powder magazine had by some carelessness been blown up. The remains showed what beautiful masonry the ancients were capable of, and the good cement they used to use. The flat bricks were so firmly bound together that in attempting to detach them from one another they broke in pieces. There are still several Christian churches in the town, the largest being the Armenian cathedral, and the greater number of the mosques were also at one time churches.

The latest appropriation of a church for a mosque occurred some forty years ago. The then governor of Diarbekr lived within the town, instead of as at present in the new serai which is about a quarter of a mile outside the walls. One day when he was in a bad temper he heard the sound of singing and chanting in this church, and was much annoyed by it. He sent to find out the reason of the noise, and was told that the Armenians were celebrating a festival; he gave orders that they should not let themselves be heard outside their church. As the noise did not cease, he sent a party of soldiers to clear the worshippers out of their church, and turned it into the mosque.

Besides the churches belonging to the Eastern Christians and Roman Catholics there is a Protestant one which is that of a congregation originally founded by the American missionaries, but of which the present pastor is an Armenian gentleman, Mr. Boyajàn. Mr. Boyajàn has spent much time in both America and England, is married to an English wife, and altogether is so Anglicised that constantly in conversation we forgot altogether that he was an Armenian and spoke to him of his countrymen as if he was one of ourselves. He, when we were there, was engaged in a dispute with the Armenian Archbishop which did not redound greatly to the credit of the latter. Mr. Boyajàn had married a man and a woman of his congregation, and the marriage did not turn out happily. The woman preferred to her lawful spouse one of the flock of the Archbishop, who, willing to insult the Protestants, said that her previous marriage was null and void, and married her to her new lover. The matter was reported to Constantinople, and

both sides had to give their version to the
government. An order was sent to the Archbishop that the woman and her new husband
were to be separated until the legal question
had been settled. He did not comply with
this order although he admitted to our consul,
Major Trotter, that he had received it. He
was afterwards asked in the council of his own
church, why he had not obeyed, when he
denied having received the order, although
he allowed that he had told the English
consul that he had. Telegrams were going
backwards and forwards on this matter whilst
we were at Diarbekr, and it had not been
settled when we left.

Owing to this, some of his priests had
blamed him for his conduct, out of seven
belonging to his cathedral five were against,
and two for, him, and the dispute waxed so
high that he and his adherents came to blows
with their opponents, and although fewer in
number drove them out of the cathedral by
force. The Armenian Archbishop and the

Syrian Bishop both came to pay us a visit
at the same time, and the Syrian, who spoke
French, had to act as interpreter for the
Armenian. The Armenian, notwithstanding
the stories about him, was a noble-looking man,
over six feet in height, and his picturesque
dress became him admirably; whilst the Syrian,
who was not of the same commanding stature,
was characterised by a look of mild benevolence.

The Armenian commenced conversation by
extolling the services that 'the church to which
he belonged had rendered to Christianity in
general, by forming a rampart against the
power of Islam, and recounting how much
it had suffered in loss of freedom and property, and how many persons it had contributed
to the glorious roll of martyrs; and arguing
therefrom that a great debt was due to the
Armenians by the Western Church. The
Syrian Bishop translated all this faithfully,
and then added, that he could not allow the
Armenians to claim all the glory, and that
indeed the Syrians had both suffered and

done more for the cause of Christianity, than
their rivals.   The Syrian Church had spread
under the Apostle Thomas to the distant
shores of India, and to the sandy deserts of
Arabia; and had possessed bishops and priests
too numerous to count, indeed that they had
been a widespreading Church embracing many
nations; that the ruins of their churches,
convents and schools were to be seen everywhere in the portion of the globe which
had accepted their teaching; whilst the
Armenian Church had never spread beyond
the limits of the nation.   The positions of
the two were now different; the Armenians
were comparatively rich and powerful, whilst
the Syrians, who had outnumbered them ten
to one, were now reduced to a mere handful;
all their worldly possessions were lost, and
their cathedrals and churches ruined.   Besides
these two dignitaries of the Eastern Church
we were also visited by the Roman Catholic
missionaries, and Mr. Boyajàn was constantly
about the consulate, his knowledge of English

always rendering him a welcome and useful guest.

Mr. Boyajàn was a member of the mejliss, or council, which, as Diarbekr is the residence of a Wali, forms a sort of court of appeal for the whole vilayet. The members of this court were supposed to receive two hundred and fifty piastres a month, or about two pounds sterling, if paid in silver. This wretched pittance was months in arrears, and paid in *caimé*, which was tumbling down at such an alarming pace, as to threaten to become almost as worthless as the *assignats* of the revolution. According to Mr. Boyajàn, his colleagues, who were mostly poor men, used to eke out their miserable salaries by receiving bribes in the most open and barefaced manner possible to conceive. If a suitor came before them he was, before being allowed to state his case, asked what he brought in his hand, and unless he had something to give had no chance of a hearing. It is only due to them to state that the bribes were in many cases very small. If a peasant came with some

complaint, they would tell him if he could not
give a lira they would be content with beshliks,
if he could not give a beshlik that they would
be content with piastres, and that if he had no
money at all, they would be content with a
lamb, a bag of flour, a fowl, or even a few eggs.
Of course in a court constituted of men who
openly sold their decisions, justice was not
obtainable except through the influence of Mr.
Boyajàn, and one or two other members who,
by their position, were above the necessity of
taking bribes, and who did what they could
to make the decisions of the court accord with
justice and reason.

The cadi at Diarbekr, whilst we were
there, was the person who had been sent as
envoy to Shere Ali by the Sultan of Turkey,
to prevent the Ameer siding with the Russians. The cadi seemed to have been much
pleased with the attention he had received in
British India; and wore on his forefinger a fine
diamond ring, which had been given him by
the Governor of Bombay. This ring we were

told to notice before he came, and compliment
him about, as he was very proud of it.   He
put the hand on which he·wore it so well to the
front that it was easy to see that he wished
us to speak about it, and thus afforded a good
opening to conversation, after the usual com-
pliments had passed between us.

The cadi had been sent to Diarbekr as a
kind of honorary exile, as he was a friend
and adherent of Midhat Pasha, and his presence
at Constantinople was feared by Khairedine
Pasha, who when he came into power got all
of those whom he expected to oppose him,
against whom anything could be said, sent into
exile, whilst those whose character was too high,
or who were too powerful to be actually exiled,
he appointed to official posts in distant parts
of the empire, so as to remove them from the
vicinity of the Sultan, for fear their influence
might be more powerful than that of himself
and his party.

We employed our time at Diarbekr by

walking round the walls, and through the
bazaars. The latter were very interesting, Diarbekr being famous for its manufactures. Very
pretty stuffs made of a mixture of cotton and
silk are woven there, and its leather is renowned
throughout Asiatic Turkey. One bazaar was
entirely occupied by jewellers, and silversmiths
who are very skilful workers in filagree, and
also inlay silver with black steel which forms
a very striking and handsome contrast. Many
old silver ·· snuff-boxes and *bonbonières* of
European manufacture are used for this latter
purpose, some of the patterns are Oriental and
good, but often much skilful work is thrown
away in copying debased modern patterns, and
wretched engravings of famous buildings.

One afternoon as we returned to Major
Trotter's he met us at the door and said,
"We have got an afternoon visitor," and on
going into the room we found an Englishman
there. This was Captain Stewart of the 11th
Hussars, who was spending his winter's leave in

travelling. He had come down the Danube
and visited Constantinople, whence he had
come by steamer to Samsoun, and had ridden
down thence by Kharput. He was now
bound for Orfa, and Aleppo, and we were
delighted to find that we should have him as
a companion as far as the former place.

He was a capital linguist, and a great
traveller, the difficulty was to find where he
had not been. He knew China well, had
travelled through Siberia and Russia, and
across North America, and wherever he had
been had noticed all that was worthy of remark.
He is now one of the military vice-consuls in
Asiatic Turkey, and it would be difficult to
have found a better man for the post.

He remained one day to rest at Diarbekr,
and then we started together. Trotter accompanied us some way out on the road, and before
parting promised if possible to meet me and
Schaefer at Mardin, where he was soon going
on account of an assault that had been made

on a branch establishment of the American missionaries there, at a town called Midyat.

We did not take the mountain road this time, but went by the made road, which runs round the northern end of the Kara-ja-Dagh. The road was fair in some places, but in those where it was most required it was wanting altogether, and the grading was so badly done that at one bridge over a ravine the road on one side ended abruptly twelve or fourteen feet above the level of the bridge itself.

Our journey to Orfa was accomplished without incident in four days, the roads after a spell of fine weather being much better than they were when we came up. One modern bridge over a stream which had commenced to fall into disrepair owing to want of super-vision had, however, lost six or seven feet of its roadway since we had crossed before, and seemed likely unless looked after to fall altogether.

Monsieur Martin and Gabriel came out to

meet us some distance from the town, and
insisted on our taking up our quarters at his
house, where he had cleared out a room for
us.   Gabriel who had been mournful at our
leaving him, seemed bright and happy, and the
dogs and servants were all well.

CHAPTER VII.

WE found the whole town of Orfa roused out
of its usual apathy by the news that the
Kurdish chiefs were to arrive the day after
we did, and that orders had been received
to greet them with all courtesy. From an
early hour in the morning the population
turned out *en masse*, Jews, Turks and Christians, and lined the road by which they were

expected to come, whilst the acting governor
with all his officials and our friend the Bimbashi,
left at ten in the morning to go to meet them.
At noon the garrison turned out, a troop of
dragoons, with new uniforms, but a sight to
make a cavalry officer weep, and a very smart
battalion of infantry, who would have done
credit to any army, the only lack being in
the number of officers. The company leaders
and guides seemed to know their work well,
and intervals and dressing were very well kept.
The infantry formed a guard of honour in the
court of the serai, and the cavalry went out
to swell the escort. We went up to the serai,
from the top of which we could see the road,
in order to witness the ceremony of the arrival
and reception of the rebels.

Whilst waiting we made the acquaintance of
a character; he was a negro, and coffee and
cigarette maker to all the governors of Orfa.
The poor fellow was deformed, and had lived
all his life in the serai; however, he seemed
happy, and said they might change governors

and sultans, anybody and everybody might go and come, but whoever filled the office of governor of Orfa would want coffee and cigarettes, and therefore his own future was always sure. Notwithstanding his age—he was over sixty—and deformity, he had just married a wife, whom he informed us was as beautiful as one of the Houris of Paradise but who, Martin said, was a greyheaded negress even older and more hideous than her husband. At about four o'clock the advance part of the cavalcade which escorted the Kurds, appeared. All seemed to be arranged to do them honour, and to flatter them, and when they dismounted in the courtyard of the serai, people bowed and salaamed to them as if they had been royalty. One rather telling salute was given by a number of camels encamped just outside the walls by the meidân. As the Kurds passed they were all made to rise up together, and stand till the procession had gone by, when they were again made to kneel down.

Next morning Stewart's horses being some-

what rested he left for Aleppo, taking back
with him our zaptieh, Hadji Mohammed, who
had now been a long while with us, and who
we certainly found to be the best we met in
the country. The Kurdish chiefs were not
visible during our stay, being presumably
employed in making the acquaintance of their
new wives and families, who had increased
in number and splendour since we had seen
them at Diarbekr. We saw all the officers
of the staff who were accompanying them,
including their brother the Sultan's aide-de-
camp, at Halil Bey's, where they seemed to
be enjoying themselves immensely. We also
paid another visit to the stables of the Bimbashi, to see his very handsome horses and
mares ; for one mare he said he had paid
two hundred and fifty pounds. How on his
pay he managed to feed, let alone buy them,
we could not imagine, as it was only a
thousand piastres a month, which being paid in
caimé was equal to about thirty shillings.

The day after Stewart left there was a great

commotion in the town, and a disturbance was feared owing to the action of the acting governor. The real governor who was away at Aleppo, had dismissed one of the mejliss for some default, and the acting governor had promised to reinstate him in consideration of a bribe; the character of the member who had been expelled was so bad that all classes combined together to prevent his re-appointment. The acting governor did not want to lose the bribe, and also did not want to provoke a revolt, and for a long time was unable to decide what to do. Matters were becoming very threatening, when a message came to Monsieur Martin asking him to interfere; he persuaded the acting governor not to make the appointment, on which the excitement calmed down immediately.

We engaged twelve mules belonging to a Christian of Mardin, called Yunnan or Jonas, for the whole distance to Baghdad, at eleven piastres a day each whilst on the road, and for half that sum whilst halted; and made our start

on the 9th of February for Mardin. In the
morning it was raining so hard that we
thought we should be unable to start; but it
cleared up about the middle of the day, and
we were able to get away. We had intended
If possible to march to Haran that same afternoon, but just after we quitted the town one
of the led horses got loose, and in endeavouring
to catch him a zaptieh who had been given
to us to show the road as far as Ras el Ain,
capsized his horse, and got badly shaken,
besides spraining his wrist. The poor fellow
wanted very much to go on with us, but was
quite unable to ride, so we had to take him
back to the serai and ask for another. An
Arab was given us, Hamed by name, who said
he knew the road well. In consequence of this
delay we had to halt for the night at a village,
Sultan Abed, where the headman said he was
brother to Martin, and that as we were friends
of Martin, he would also be a brother to us.
He however charged for use of house and
stables, and all the food we wanted, and would

not let us light a fire in a fire-place in the room
we slept in for fear of spoiling his whitewash.

Next day we reached Haran, which shows
signs of its ancient importance, though now
only inhabited by half nomad Arabs, who have
villages of dirty conical huts built out of old
Roman bricks. Close to the well of Rebekah—
or what is said to be the well of Rebekah—
are the remains of a very large church and
monastery. The church tower is still in pretty
good preservation, and forms a famous land-
mark for a very long distance round. The
lower half of the tower is built of stone carefully
cut and squared, whilst the upper portion is
built of bricks, from which the plaster with
which they were covered has been worn away
by the weather, and the lower corners of this
brick part are also broken away, giving it the
appearance of being balanced on the lower half.
The way Cleopatra's Needle now stands on its
pedestal on the Thames Embankment gives one
precisely the same idea. Near the ancient town
are remains of mounds and earthworks which

look like a Roman camp, whilst the town itself
used to be surrounded by a well-built stone
wall, with square bastions at regular intervals.
At one corner of this wall stands the castle or
citadel, which is still in a good state of preservation ; part is used as a habitation by the
people, and other parts for a khan, stables, and
granaries. We were lodged in a large circular
upper chamber with a domed roof, and arched
windows like embrasures. Round this room
were ranged huge cylindrical earthen jars, in
which their winter store of grain was kept by
our hosts. Another part of the citadel was
much like a Norman keep. A large circular
building surrounded a courtyard, in the centre
of which was a very solid stone tower or *donjon*.
The Roman camp was probably built by the
Romans under Julian, as it was here that he
divided his forces into two columns, one of
which, under his own orders was to advance
by the line of the Euphrates, depending on
his fleet for supplies ; whilst the other, under
the command of Procopius and Sebastian was

to advance by way of Nisibin, and descending the banks of the Tigris, join their emperor under the walls of Ctesiphon. The failure of this second column of thirty thousand men to fulfil their task, caused also the failure of Julian's projects.

The stone walls, church, and castle are no doubt the work of the Christians under the orders of the Counts of Orfa, but who used the old Roman town as a quarry for bricks ; much of the stonework being lined with Roman bricks, which were also used to pave the floors of some of the rooms in the castle.

Here I measured a base, and made a fair start for triangulating from Orfa where I had made a station on the top of Monsieur Martin's house, whence the church tower of Haran was plainly visible.

In the morning we were delighted to find that rain, which had been falling for the most part of the two previous days, had ceased, but a thick fog prevented our starting till late in the forenoon. As the fog lifted we could see all around us flocks of kettah and plover, but they were all very shy, and we could not get within shot. . About noon we came upon some gazelle, and for a long time these seemed as wary as the feathered game ; but at last we managed to get within about forty yards of a solitary one before she saw us, and we slipped the greyhounds. A short course ot a hundred yards and it was all over, Saada rolling over with the gazelle, and Richan and Nimshi coming up a second or two afterwards. The poor beast was dead before we could dismount, and greyhounds do worry the meat terribly.

Soon after we came to a well, where we found two men and a camel who had halted there in hopes that we might have a cord long enough to draw water, and from them we learnt that although we had taken the precaution of getting a guide at Haran to show us our first night's camping-place, we had come much too far to the south.

Leaving the well, we entered low rolling hills

and passed by a couple of camps and some
ancient quarries and caves.   Our Arab from
Haran said that in these caves in ancient days,
Christian hermits used to live, but how long ago
he did not know.   He was again soon at a loss
for his direction, and we rather gave up hope of
finding the ruined city where we were to halt.
At about four o'clock we saw a large number
of camels, and vast flocks of sheep and goats,
and sitting on the grass near a large square
building some half-dozen men with their horses
tethered by their sides.   As we approached they
mounted and rode towards us, when we found
they were the chief men of a party of nomad
Kurds who were moving in search of pasture
for their animals.

As far as we could see in either direction
there were flocks, each separate flock following
its own shepherd.   They told us they were
marching for water which lay to the south-
east, whilst the city of the Nabiy Shiab which
we were looking for lay north-east and some
distance away ; but on the road there we should

'find some Arab camps where we should be able to halt.

The building which we had seen was evidently one of the forts built in the country during the sway of Baldwin and his successors, as the sign of the cross occurred on several of the stones. Outside was a large stone tank which was now choked with sand and earth, and inside the enceinte was a blocked-up well.

Bidding good-bye to the Kurds we rode on in the direction they had pointed out, anxiously looking for signs of either the ruins or tents of Arabs. Large numbers of the middle-sized bustard kept tantalising us; time after time did we stalk patiently after them, and just as we flattered ourselves we were going to get within rifle range they would get up and fly about four or five hundred yards further off.

We were almost despairing of ever finding a place to camp, when just at sunset we saw the ruins of which we were, in search in front of us. When we got there we found that an Arab camp had been there that morning, but now all

was deserted. The ruins above ground were
nothing remarkable, being only what one might
expect to find if a modern eastern town were
deserted by its inhabitants, and allowed to fall
into ruins. But beneath these insignificant ruins
were a number of large caves hewn in the solid
rock, which had served as habitations to the
followers of the prophet after whom the place
was named.

We took possession of one which was dry
and clean, and others were speedily appropriated
by the muleteers for themselves and their
animals. Suddenly, whilst we were all busily
arranging things for the night, we heard dread-
ful cries and shrieks from the one the muleteers
had chosen for their bedroom. On going there,
we found that the youngest muleteer, a lad of
sixteen or seventeen, had been left there by
himself to prepare matters, whilst the others
were busy about the mules. Suddenly the
candle he had lit had been extinguished, and
something soft and fluffy brushed against his
face. He rushed out screaming, and declared

that the devil was there, and that he would not go back again. All his friends were as frightened as he was, and no one would go in; so I got a light, and on entering the place found that a poor little owlet, who was as frightened as the boy, had been the cause of the whole business; having been disturbed by the light he had tried to fly out of the cave, and passing by the candle had knocked it out with his wing.

The devil having been laid, we soon made ourselves comfortable, and the night in a cave was by no means the worst I have passed.

Next morning before starting we inspected the cave which had served as a mosque to Nabiy Shiab, and his sleeping cell, where a rude couch had been cut out of the rock, with a spring trickling close by its head. This spring was said to be miraculous, only running in dry weather when water was scarce elsewhere, and ceasing entirely when it was abundant.

Here we picked up the proper track to Ras el Ain, and went along more confidently; our guide from Haran returning to his own

home abundantly satisfied by the gift of a
medjidie (about four shillings) for his long
walk.

We went through an undulating country,
passing the sites of several Arab camps and
two or three small ruined forts, but seeing no
sign of life till about two in the afternoon,
when, from behind a hillock, there appeared
a Bedouin who was shortly followed by three
others. There then ensued a sort of skirmish-
ing approach, as they alternately retreated and
advanced, until at last they were within hailing
distance, and inquiries were made by both parties as to their respective intentions. When
they heard we were English, they said it was
all right, and came up to us; and with all the
frankness imaginable said they were detached
from a body of eighty horsemen who were
going to make a ghazou or raid on the Kurds
we had seen the day before. When they left,
our zaptieh urged us to make haste to get
out of their neighbourhood, as perhaps they
might change their intentions, and make their

attack on us, instead of on their hereditary
foes the Kurds.

We travelled on till sunset, passing many
places where hewn stones seemed to indicate
the sites of ancient cities, when we camped near
a pool of water remaining in the bed of a
watercourse. Next morning we were on the
move by daylight, and were much astonished
to find that a party of some twenty horsemen
had camped within three hundred yards of us ;
the footmarks of their horses showed that
they had taken the road we were to follow,
so that it was necessary that we should march
with all due caution. Very probably they had
no evil intentions towards us, but their having
camped without any fire was a sign that they
were looking for some enemy, and were not
on a peaceful expedition. About an hour after
we left camp, their tracks turned off to the
south, and as on following them for some
distance we could see nothing of them,
we concluded that most probably they were
friends of those we had met the day before,

and were going to assist them against the Kurds.

In the middle of the day our zaptieh, who seemed very nervous, and was galloping about looking out for Arabs or Circassians, came and told us that there were a hundred horsemen behind a small hill he had ridden up, and that they were sure to attack us. We soon saw a small party of twenty people or thereabouts, on foot, driving laden donkeys and bullocks, which he wished to make out were mounted Arabs, and when I told him I could see through my glasses what they were, said that the horsemen must still be hidden. Shortly after we saw some people in the direction he pointed out as that in which the horsemen were, and as the mirage was very strong we could not make them out for some time. At last we found that they were a small party of Kurds, an old man and an older woman, two hobbledehoys, a boy and a girl, with all their possessions packed on two bullocks, a cow, and three donkeys which they drove before them, whilst they were followed by three dogs.

From them we learnt that the Arabs we had seen the day before were Adwân Arabs, and that the Adwân had shortly before made a raid on a party of Aneizeh and stolen seven horses, and that now Adwân and Aneizeh were dodging each other about the country. We gave them a small present, and as our zaptieh was evidently all adrift about the road, got them to put us right. About an hour after we had quitted them, the zaptieh said he recognised a hill, and that Ras el Ain was close to it; as he said he was perfectly sure that he was right we followed his lead, when luckily I saw the town away to our left, and we changed our direction for it. As we approached, the town seemed to fade away, but as we were close to a camp of semi-nomad Arabs, who had their tents on a mound near some ancient canals, we went there and asked them to tell us the right way. We found that we were now going right, and after passing

over a small rise in the ground saw Ras el Ain
a short way in front of us.   By a most curious
effect of mirage the vision of the town had
been refracted into the air above the rise,
which would, in ordinary circumstances, have
hidden it from us completely.

We soon came upon a party of mounted
Circassians armed with guns and swords, who
were escorting half a dozen bullock carts to
another settlement about ten miles off, as they
lived in such constant enmity with the Arabs
that they were afraid even to go that small
distance except in a large number and well
armed.

Close by where we met them was one of the
sources which give the name of Ras el Ain
(head of the springs) to the place, and which are
the principal headwaters of the River Khabour.
It was a large pool about a hundred yards in
diameter, and all round springs were gushing
out of the soil, whilst on one side a large
stream left which, uniting with others coming
from similar pools, forms the river.   The water

was of a crystal clearness which I have never seen excelled, and many fish were swimming about.

In another half hour we arrived in the town of Ras el Ain, which, though only built about twenty years ago, is already falling into ruins, and is much too large for its rapidly decreasing population.

The Kaimacan was absent, and it was with some difficulty that we found lodgings; we were warned not to pitch our tent and picket our horses for fear of being robbed by the Circassians; at last we got hold of a sergeant of zaptieh and made him open some rooms and stables in the serai where we could secure ourselves against thieves.

CHAPTER VIII.

Ras el Ain is the ancient Resaina, and principally famous as the scene of a battle in which
Timesitheus, the father-in-law of the Emperor
Gordian, defeated the Persian monarch Sapor
in A.D. 242. In later times, and especially
since the days of Mohammed, it had been
almost lost to sight, until the Turkish government determined to settle some of the

Circassians, expelled from their country by the Russians, on the spot.

Being far away from the habitations of settled agriculturists, although good soil and water abound, it was hoped that there would be no difficulty in forming a prosperous colony of these exiles, who might also be expected to form a sort of outpost which would defend the cultivated lands of more northern Mesopotamia from the inroads of the Arabs of the plains.

The Circassians were transported with all their goods and chattels from the coast of the Black Sea, by the animals and vehicles of the inhabitants, who had also to provide them with food. During their transit through Kurdistan they managed to make themselves so hated by the Kurds, that the families who settled round Diarbekr have been almost destroyed by the constant feuds waged between them and the original inhabitants.

Like those who are now pouring into Syria, the Circassians, trusting to superior arms and organisation, robbed and ill-treated their

neighbours, till the latter, obtaining no redress
at the hands of their rulers, took the matter into
their own, and whenever they had an opportunity shot the Circassians from lurking places in
the rocks and mountains.

Here at Ras el Ain they had not so utterly
vanished, but their power was rapidly waning;
they had indeed for some time kept the Arabs
back, but the sheep dogs had proved worse
than the wolves, and the inhabitants of the
villages in the plains below Mardin regarded
them with more aversion than they did their
ancient foes the Arabs, who were possessed
of principles of honour, whilst the highest
boast of a Circassian is that he is a thief,
and he will not even scruple to rob his
guests.

Between the Arabs and Circassians it has
always been open war, and the Circassians are
now having the worst of it. At first when they
were supplied with arms and ammunition by
the Turkish Government, they had driven the
Arabs back; but now, with rapidly diminishing

numbers and lacking supplies, they cannot hold
their own, and if their own story is to be
believed, had lost in the twelve months pre-
ceding our visit, over one hundred men in fights
with the Shammar Arabs. Illness and disease
were also rapidly carrying them off, and the
graveyards near occupied far more space than
the town itself, though it was far too large for
its shrunken population.

A boy *sous-officier*, with a face that looked
as if it had been carved out of a tallow candle,
was apparently the chief person in the town,
and was very officious. Before he would give
us a zaptieh to show the road to Mardin he
demanded to see our firman, and being "dressed
in a little brief authority," tried to make the
most of his importance. He said he had been
educated at the Military Academy at Constantinople, and had learnt both French and English,
but his knowledge of one was limited to the
alphabet, and of the other to two words
which need not be repeated. Our Orfa
zaptieh refused to go any further with us, as

his horse was tired out, and therefore we had
to get others from this lout.

The Circassians, although they rob very
indiscriminately, have some sort of terror of
the powers that be, and are said never to
attack parties that are accompanied even by
one zaptieh, so although for some reasons we
would sooner be without chance zaptieh of
whom we knew nothing, we thought it was
best to take them.

We had people coming in to stare at us all
the evening, and smoking and making remarks
in the rudest way whilst we were having our
supper ; indeed they became such a nuisance
that I was compelled to tell the *sous-officier*,
that if he did not manage matters a little better
I should report him at Mardin, and get him
punished.

The river which flowed by the town was full
of fish, so as it was still early when we came in,
I put my rod together and tried several different
flies and also an artificial minnow, but without
any success, probably owing to the very great

clearness of the water. The people had never
seen a rod used before, though they catch
many fish with nets and traps, and of course we
were followed by a noisy mob, who may have
contributed to my want of success.

In the 'morning we started again, glad to
leave the inhospitable neighbourhood of the
Circassians. Close to the town we passed some
more great pools, fed by springs like the one
we had seen the day before, but here ancient
dykes and dams showed that they had once
been used for irrigation, though at present there
is scarcely any cultivation.

There were a few Arab camps about, the
inhabitants of which observe a sort of armed
neutrality towards the Circassians. They had
come from their usual grazing grounds to the
neighbourhood of the streams on account of the
failure of water, as owing to the winter rains
being less than usual, much of the country was
suffering from drought. At one of these places
our greyhounds made a dash into the middle
of a flock of lambs, and rolled one over, though

without hurting it. An old hag who was near
came rushing up and abused and swore at us
vigorously, telling us we were no sportsmen
to allow our dogs to hunt sheep when there
were plenty of gazelles in the country for
us and our dogs. A small present caused her
to change her tone altogether, and she asked
us to the tents to drink milk; as it was still
early we refused, and rode on.

At about eleven we came to a large camp,
where the Kaimacan of Ras el Ain was staying
with some Kurds. He had a large escort of
Circassians who had a sort of military bearing.
Their long single-breasted frock coats, all cut
on precisely the same pattern, and which were
brown, red, or blue, had a uniform appearance
to which the cartridge pockets sewn on their
breasts contributed not a little. They all wore
sheepskin caps, loose white trousers, and black
boots reaching to the knee. Round their waists,
as usual, a belt with a perfect armoury of pistols
and daggers, some of which were very handsome,
and they all carried their guns slung in cases

across their shoulders. It seemed as if with
drill and discipline they might be made into
good troops, but those who undertake the
task will have to be men of firm will and
prompt action.

The Kaimacan was sitting in the tent of
the Kurdish chief, and said he wearied for
Stamboul and its pleasures; he had a tired
and wearied expression, and was very thank-
ful for any news that we could give him,
as he said that at Ras el Ain they were often
three and four months without hearing anything of the outer world.

After coffee we went on again, passing by
some small Circassian encampments which were
all situated on streams or near springs, whilst
occasionally we saw in the distance large camps
of Kurds and Arabs.

We came upon enormous herds of gazelle,
they were literally in hundreds, but though
we had some very good runs the greyhounds
could do nothing with them. Sultan carried
me magnificently, and I several times rode past

both the greyhounds and the gazelles so as
to turn the latter back, but it was of no use.
The dogs were not wanting in pluck, but in
speed, as they ran till they could actually run
no further. We might have shot some of the
gazelle if it had not been that we were so
elated by the greyhounds having killed one
the day we left Haran that we were determined
they should repeat the feat if possible.

At night we camped near a small hamlet of
Circassians with whom some Arabs who had
lost nearly all their cattle had made friends.
Our zaptieh from Ras el Ain told us that both
Arabs and Circassians were thieves, as it was
only the most degraded of Arabs who ever
made friends with the Circassians, and therefore a good watch must be kept, and they
themselves would not sleep a wink during the
night. Not expecting this to be quite likely,
we divided all our people into watches, so that
a look-out might be kept upon our neighbours.

In the middle of the night I fancied I heard
a noise, and going out found the whole lot

buried in slumber and Sultan missing from
the line of horses.   I went back into the tent
and got my revolver and woke Schaefer, then
kicking up the zaptieh I went with one up
towards the Arabs' tents.   There every one
pretended to be asleep also, but I found Sultan
behind their camp; the pegs of both his head
and heel ropes had been pulled up, but on
rousing the Arabs out, they of course declared
that they knew nothing about it, and that the
horse must have got loose by himself. As
I had found my horse I did not much care,
but I told them that any one found near our
animals before daylight would be fired on, and
that if they wished to indulge in nocturnal
rambles they had better choose some other
direction.

When daylight appeared we were not sorry
to get away from our neighbours, who were
only lacking in power, certainly not in will,
to be troublesome.

Close by this village was a graveyard in
which I counted over a hundred graves, though

there are only seven houses and the place had only been founded fifteen years. Our road lay nearly the whole way along a line of deserted villages which had been built along the banks of a stream coming from the hills near Mardin, and which we afterwards heard had all been inhabited by Christians prior to the arrival of the Circassians in the country.

On and about this stream were numerous wildfowl, and we got a few duck. There were also great flocks of bustard and numerous herds of gazelle, but both were too wily to allow us to get within range. Several *tels*, or small hills, were scattered about marking the sites of ancient cities, which either took advantage of a natural hill on which to build their citadel or else constructed an artificial one for the purpose.

Some of these I used for points in the triangulation, and on one I had chosen we saw some horsemen who were evidently watching our movements. At first I thought that perhaps Trotter might have got to Mardin a day or two before that appointed for our rendezvous there, and have come out to meet us. This was strengthened by my thinking that no one but an Englishman would take the, trouble to go up to the top of a hill whilst the road was level, and seeing that two horses were roans which I knew was the colour of both his.

As we got nearer I saw they were Circassians; and one zaptieh, whom I had taken with me to hold my horse whilst I was taking my angles, tried hard to dissuade me from going up. He, when he saw that I was determined, said he would not go with me, and tried to bolt, but I caught his horse's bridle and said that he was under my orders and must do what I told him. Grumbling and growling very much at the mad English he went up to the top with me, where we were confronted by three Circassians with levelled guns, whilst another held their horses.

I said "*Salaam Aleikoum*," and they surlily replied "*Aleikoum Salaam*," still keeping their guns pointing at us. I asked what they were afraid of, and they said they had thought that we were soldiers sent out to take them prisoners and they were determined to resist. I assured them that nothing was further from my thought than thief-catching, and that if they did not molest us we would not hurt them; on this they mounted their horses and rode away, and I could see they went off to join another party of five or six who were hidden in a ruined village near. Three of the men were hideous Tchetchen or Tartar Circassians, whilst the fourth was a handsome Tcherkess or true Circassian. The last was leader and spokesman of the party.

After taking my angles I rode after the caravan, and Yunnan, the muleteer, told me when I described the men that he knew them to be part of a band of robbers who had once attacked a caravan in which he was, and had been driven off with loss of one or two of their number.

Thinking it as well to be prepared in case they should come with their friends to attack us, we gave our spare guns to the most trustworthy of our people, and determined to remain close to the mules. The two zaptieh were evidently of an opinion that they would not be safe near the caravan, and speedily put half a mile of distance between themselves and it, so as to have a good chance of escape in case it should be attacked.

We did not come up to them again till we reached a ford near a village, where we found them washing themselves, having picketed their horses to their rifles, which they had shoved into rat-holes, of which the river banks were full. They now assured us that they had been riding on in front so as to be able to give us warning if the Circassians were coming, but as they had carefully kept the caravan between themselves, and the direction in which the robbers had been last seen, we did not put much faith in their assurances.

Round the village, which was a very small

one, were some remains of old columns and other ruins, over which the sheep and goats of the villagers were straying.

We now saw two high towers, which we were told were at the village where we were to halt for the night, and rode straight for them across a cultivated and fertile plain. When we got near, the two towers proved to be part of a very large and ancient mosque, in the middle of a Mohammedan village, beyond which, and separated from it by an open space of about five or six hundred yards, was a Christian village.

As all our people were Christians, with the exception of the two zaptieh, we rode on to the Christian village, which we found was called Tel Armen, and where the whole population turned out to welcome us cordially. A widow-woman, who kept a khan, begged us to lodge there, and we promised to do so, but we had not been there five minutes before one of the two Priests, Dom Gabriel, came to beg us to accept the shelter of their house. As the

loads were already off the mules we thought
it best to stop where we were, more especially
as our hostess implored us to remain, but. we
said we would go up to the Priests' house
as soon as we had seen our horses stabled
and fed.

A second priest, Dom Jacques, soon appeared,
who·talked French, which he said he had learnt
at the Jesuit college at Beirut.   He apologised
for not having come to meet us, but seeing
people coming from the direction of Ras el Aïn
he was afraid lest they should prove to be
Circassians, and he had hastened to hide his
horse in the cellar, as a few months before
a party of robbers had stolen a very valuable
mare belonging to him.

We went up with the Priests to their house,
where we found them comfortably, though
rudely, lodged, and had a long conversation
with them.   They were working under the
orders of the Mission at Mosul, and had been
very successful, as they. had not only induced
most of the native Christians to acknowledge

the authority of the Pope, but had also converted several Mohammedans.

Great jealousy existed in the neighbouring
villages, and there were constant disputes, but
some of the Kurds were their friends and
would come to their assistance in serious
matters, and in the lesser affairs they could
shelter themselves in their village. About
six months before our arrival, however, they
had had a great fright, as a pitched battle took
place between two thousand of the people
who were friendly to them, and the same
number of their enemies, just in front of the
village. For a long time the result was
doubtful, but luckily their friends were victorious, and all they had to do was to tend
the wounded and feed the victors and their
horses.

They complained bitterly of the injustice
of the tax - collectors, who, according to
them, often eased the inhabitants of neighbouring villages at their expense. Only a few
weeks before, after all their taxes were

supposed to be paid, a fresh levy. had been made on them of eight piastres for every man, woman, and child, in the village, and many of the poorer families had to sell their property to meet this unexpected claim.

The ruins we had seen near the ford,-they told us, marked the site of an ancient Chaldean city where a synod had once been held, which was attended by over two hundred bishops. When we left their house they accompanied us back to the khan, and sat talking with us for a long time. The average number of camels, they told us, that passed by daily was over five hundred. Over a thousand were camped between the two villages, besides mules and a large number of pilgrims, of whom several thousands passed by in the course of the year.

One inconvenience which we found. from being in a Christian village was that all our servants got drunk, liquor being cheap and plentiful. Daher, the groom, was very pious in his cups, and asked the Priests what the

price of a mass for his father's soul would
be, and finding that it was only five piastres,
paid for one ; the remainder of the money he
had in his pocket, ten piastres, he spent in
raki, and soon was reduced to a quiescent·
state.

Next morning Dom Jacques, and a large
number of the villagers, accompanied us for
some two or three miles on the way to Mardin,
when they turned back, as they did not dare
to go any farther on account of the next
village being hostile.

We soon after arrived at the foot of the
mountains on which Mardin is situated, which
rise abruptly from the northern edge of the
great Mesopotamian plain.

They mark some great natural convulsion ;
being composed of very much contorted
igneous rocks at the base, whilst the summits
are of the same geological formation as the
plain.

We rode up, by a winding, steep, and rocky
path, but we soon found it better to dismount

and to scramble up by means of our own feet
and hands.

Just outside the town were the houses of the
American Mission, where we found Trotter
had arrived two days before, and were kindly
welcomed by its members.

CHAPTER IX.

THE American Mission was very different
from that of the Priests' at Tel Armen,
houses built on a European or American
model, and furnished so as to correspond with
their architecture. Dr. Thom, Mr. Dewy,
their wives, and two young ladies, form the
Mission party; and they seem to have made
themselves very comfortable. They have,
besides their dwelling-houses, a good building
which fills the double purpose of school and

chapel. Native teachers assist in secular education, and besides work indoors, teach agriculture on a piece of land close by the school.

The Mission has a summer residence a short way from Mardin, where its members are not so exposed to the burning rays of the summer sun as they would be in the town, which, facing due south, and standing on a steep slope, must be a regular furnace in July and August. They have also established a branch at a small town called Midyat, and it was principally on account of a disturbance that had taken place there that Trotter had come to Mardin, as the American Missionaries are all under English protection where there are no consuls of their own nationality.

One of the young lady teachers was alone at Midyat when the affair took place, and several stones were flung at the house she was living in, and one struck her on the back of the head, though without doing her any damage, owing to the thickness of her back hair.

The whole business seemed to have origi-
nated in a very small matter. The Kaimacan
had promised that when the Protestants had
to furnish anything to government, the order
should be sent to the vakil, or representative
of the missionaries. On one occasion this had
not been done, and he told the persons who
had been ordered to supply food or bedding
for the accommodation of some stranger passing through the town, not to do so until he
had seen the authorities, and ascertained if the
order was correct. The people who were
carrying out the order stirred up a disturbance
against him, and he ran for his house, the
upper part of which formed the Mission
quarters. He got in all safe, and the people
were soon dispersed, but not till they had done
some damage by throwing stones. We asked
the young lady who was there at the time if
she did not feel afraid, to which she replied,
" Oh, no ! I had my seven-shooter ready, and
if any had broke in I guess I should have
fired."

The vakil was now at Mardin, and Trotter
was going, as soon as he had settled a few
matters at Mardin, to Midyat, with him and
Dr. Thom, to investigate the whole matter.
As they could, by making a ·small détour, accompany us as far as Nisibin, it was arranged
that we should all start together.

The chief lions of Mardin are its citadel,
which dominates the whole surrounding country,
and a Saracenic doorway which is said to be
one of the finest, if not the finest, remnant of
Saracen art in Asiatic Turkey.   Both these we
visited, and the doorway was certainly very
fine indeed.   The citadel, situated on the top-
most crags of the mountain, could only be
reached by a road as steep as the Nix
Mangiare Stairs at Malta, up and down which
the ladies· cantered their horses quite uncon-
cernedly.

From the top a view could be had of the
whole surrounding country ; to the north the
limit was the snowy mountains of Armenia,
whilst on the southern horizon we could see

the Sinjar mountains and the Abdul Aziz
range, which is really a continuation of the
Sinjar. The volcanic cone of Kaukab, standing in the plain to the south-east, showed
where the subterranean forces which had
raised the range on which Mardin stands had
found a vent. The whole plain was covered
with small *tels*, near each of which, in ancient
days, had been prosperous towns. Now, although the whole is capable of cultivation,
there are only a few scattered villages, and the
number of these is even now decreasing.

The citadel has undergone various sieges,
and was captured by Chosroes the Second in
A.D. 606; and is reported to have been one
of the few places which resisted the victorious
arms of Tamerlane.

It is related that the great victor, unable to
make any impression on the fortifications,
determined to reduce it by famine. Months
elapsed, and to all his summons to surrender the garrison returned a brave defiance.
At last when almost all their stores were

exhausted, and starvation was staring them in the face, they bethought them of a stratagem.

A litter of puppies had lately been born in the citadel, so they milked the mother, and with the milk they made a cheese. A few grains of wheat and barley had fallen unperceived near the well from which they drew their water, these had sprung up and borne fruit and ripened. With this fresh grain they made flour, which was made into a cake; and when the heralds of Tamerlane made, as was their daily custom, a demand for the surrender of the place, the garrison flung down from the walls the cheese and the cake, saying, " Go, ask your master if he has better bread or fresher cheese than this we can afford to throw away." The heralds when they returned to their sovereign, gave him the bread and cheese, and told him the message which was given with them. Despairing of reducing a place which was apparently so well provisioned, Tamerlane raised the siege and marched away.

Mardin has now a population of about

twenty thousand, of whom half are Mohammedans, the remainder, with the exception of
twenty or thirty Jews, are Christians. About
five thousand are Eastern Christians, who have
acknowledged the supremacy of the Pope, and
who are looked after by Roman Catholic missionaries; three hundred are Protestants; and
the remainder are Eastern Christians who retain their independence in religious matters.
Situated on the road which is usually followed
by travellers, between Mosul and Diarbekr,
it is a place of some importance, and its vineyards and fruit-gardens are famous in all the
surrounding country.

Trotter having completed his business at
Mardin, we started with him and Dr. Thom
on the morning of the 19th of February.
We left the town by a much better road than
the series of rock ladders by which we had
climbed up, and which, though it would be
abused in any European country, was the
best piece of made road we had seen since
leaving the coast. All the members of the

Mission accompanied us some little way out of
the town, acting on the motto of "Welcome
the coming, speed the parting guest."

When we got down on the plains, Trotter
and I had a race, in order to determine the
respective merits of his horse Dervish, and my
Sultan; Dr. Thom joined in with a very good
little horse, but he could not keep up with us.
After a good race I had decidedly the best of
it; but as Trotter was the heavier man, he was
able to please himself by thinking that the
difference in weight had told, whilst I could
flatter myself that I had won.

Spurs from the hills ran some way out into
the plain, and on these, hares were said to be
numerous, so we spread out our line to try
and beat some up, but without success; just
as we were giving up all ideas of hares, we
saw some gazelle just on the edge of the plain,
and making for the hills. We rode carefully
across their line so as to try to head them
back, but the vakil of Dr. Thom who, though
he might be a most estimable man, was a very

inferior sportsman, unluckily rode on down below, and frightened them so that they made for
the hills ; when in another couple of minutes
we should have been between them and their
refuge, with all the greyhounds.

Four hours after leaving Mardin we arrived
at Dara, where there are many interesting
ruins ; indeed, it shows more clearly than any
other city we visited, to what a pitch Roman
engineering had arrived when they constructed
this frontier fortress.

The possession of Nisibin by the Persians
had deprived the eastern frontier of the Roman
empire of its principal defence, and when Kobad
was occupied by the invasion of the Ephthalites, Anastasius was not restrained by the
treaty signed by Isdigerd and the Emperor
Theodosius in A.D. 441, from constructing
the stronghold of Dara, though one of the
articles was that neither power should build
fortresses near the frontiers of the other.
Notwithstanding its being well known that
Dara was founded by Anastasius, the present

inhabitants, misled by the name, say that it was founded by Darius.

On the termination of his war with the Ephthalites in 517, Kobad demanded an explanation from Anastasius, who paid a large sum to the Persian monarch to forego his claims for the demolition of the fortress. Apparently the sum was not large enough, for in the following year we find him again disputing on this subject with Justin the successor of Anastasius. Internal troubles prevented the Persians from attacking their western rivals during the reign of Justin, and his nephew Justinian, seeing the importance of Dara, strengthened the place by all the means in his power. According to Gibbon "the fortifications of Dara may represent the military architecture of the age. The city was surrounded by two walls, and the interval between them, of fifty paces, afforded a retreat to the cattle of the besieged. The inner wall was a monument of strength and beauty : it measured sixty feet from the ground, and the height of the towers was one hundred

feet; the loopholes, from whence an enemy
might be annoyed with missile weapons, were
small and numerous ; the soldiers were planted
along the rampart, under the shelter of double
galleries, and a third platform, spacious and
secure, was raised on the summit of the towers.
The exterior wall appears to have been less
lofty, but more solid; and each tower was
connected by a quadrangular bulwark. A hard
rocky soil resisted the tools of the miners,
and on the south-east, where the ground was
more tractable, their approach was retarded
by a new work, which advanced in the shape
of a half-moon. The double and treble ditches
were filled with a stream of water : and in the
management of the river, the most skilful labour
was employed to supply the inhabitants, to dis-
tress the besiegers, and to prevent the mischiefs
of a natural or artificial inundation."

Dara during the sixth century occupies an
important place in the history of the East. At
the same time that Justin died, the infirmities
of Kobad prevented him from any longer taking

the field in person, and he had therefore to
entrust the conduct of his armies to his generals.
Belisarius, who was in command of the Roman
troops at Nisibin, was ordered, in A.D. 528, to
construct a new fort on the frontier, but the
Persians totally defeated the army covering
the new works, and Belisarius was forced
to take refuge within the walls of Dara.
Justinian, with unusual generosity, did not
blame his lieutenant, but on the contrary
gave him the title of Consul of the East,
and enabled him to collect an effective army
of twenty-five thousand men.   Perozes, the
Persian general, emboldened by the successes
of the last campaign, advanced to attack
Belisarius with forty thousand men.   On
arriving near Dara, the Persian general found
his opponent had posted his army so skilfully
in front of the town, that notwithstanding his
vast superiority in numbers, he determined to
wait until reinforcements from Nisibin should
reach him.   Next day, having now fifty thousand men under his command, he summoned

Belisarius to surrender, or. even if he dared to
accept the combat, to prepare breakfast and a
bath within the walls of Dara, for he would be
conqueror. The battle was waged long and
furiously with varying success, but in the evening the victory was won by the Romans, who
routed their enemies with great loss.

After the death of Kobad, his son Chosroes,
who succeeded him, made a treaty with Justinian, in A.D. 532, called "the endless peace,"
amongst the provisions of which, was one, by
which Dara was to remain a fortified post, but
was not to be made the Roman headquarters
in these regions. In 539 Chosroes broke this
treaty and carried his victorious standards as
far as the shores of the Mediterranean. After
staying a time at Antioch he returned to his
own country by a route which led past Orfa
and Dara, from each of which he demanded a
large payment, although he had signed articles
of peace with the Romans before quitting Orfa.
Confident in the strength of their fortifications,
the garrison of Dara refused compliance with

the unjust claim, and Chosroes laid siege to the place. The besiegers endeavoured by mining to find an entrance into the city, but were completely foiled by the countermines of the besieged. Chosroes now agreed to raise the siege on the payment of a thousand pounds of silver, which was .paid by the Romans, sooner than longer endure the inconveniences of a siege.

This peace was not of any long duration, but in 545, a cessation of hostilities for five years was agreed to by both sides. During this truce the Romans assert that the Persians laid a plot to seize Dara by treachery, which, being discovered, came to nothing.

War broke out again in 549, but the scene of the main struggle was in Lazistan ; and Dara was only mentioned in the treaty of peace concluded in 557, when the same rules were made regarding her as in the treaty of 532.

In 572 we find Chosroes defeating a Roman army under Marcian, who were besieging Nisibin, and forcing them to take shelter within the walls of Dara.

The hitherto maiden fortress made a bold
defence against an army of forty thousand
horse, and a hundred thousand foot; but, not
being relieved, the brave garrison had to surrender in the end of 573. Just before the death
of Chosroes, a treaty was being negotiated, by
the terms of which, Dara was to be ceded to
the Romans, but it was never concluded; and
it was reserved for his grandson and namesake
Chosroes II. to give up Dara to the Romans,
in return for the assistance rendered him by
the Emperor Maurice in regaining his throne,
from which he had been driven by the opposi-
tion of Bahram.

When Maurice was murdered by Phocas,
Chosroes made war against the latter, in order
to avenge the death of his friend and bene-
factor, in A.D. 603. The tide of war set
decidedly against the Romans, and in 605
Chosroes in person laid siege to Dara, and after
about nine months compelled it to surrender.

So much for the history of Dara. The remains
of the ancient buildings still attest its former

grandeur, though the present inhabitants are
a mere handful of agriculturists. Amongst the
most remarkable remains, were a series of ten
arched vaults, which were partly cut out of the
solid rock, and partly built of cut stones, with
string courses of flat·burnt-bricks ; these were
arched over with bricks, and plastered. The
dimensions of each were seventy feet long,
twelve feet wide, and forty feet from crown of
arch to floor ; whilst the partition walls were
two feet six inches in thickness. The people
said that these were originally water tanks, but
from their position, and the comparative slight-
ness of the walls between them, I should think
it more probable that they were granaries. A
very large square building was almost buried in
soil ; it was eighty feet square, and had rows of
square columns to support its roof, in the walls
were recesses which corresponded to the intervals between the columns. The sides faced
directly to the cardinal points ; on the western
side was a staircase by which we went down

from the present level of the ground.   In the
N.E. and S.E. corners were shafts eight feet
square which were outside the walls.   Each
row of columns was connected by arches, but
the spaces between the rows were covered by
large slabs of stone, in several courses, each
course projecting over the one below, a distance equal to the thickness of the slabs of
which it was composed, until they approached
the corresponding ones on the opposite side
sufficiently for the intervening space to be
covered by one slab.   The projecting corners
of these slabs were cut off, so that the vaulted
space between the rows of columns consisted of
two sides inclining towards each other, at an
angle of forty-five degrees, with a flat crown.
On the top of this building, were the ruins of
another, in the construction of which round
columns had been used.

North-west, some forty yards from here, was
a square tank, partly hewn out of the rock, and
partly built of stone walls, consisting of three

thicknesses of stones two feet wide, and from
six to eight feet in length.

The walls surrounding the town appear to
have been of great strength, and over where the
stream which supplied water to the garrison
flowed was a large building of carefully hewn
stones, which the present inhabitants said used
to be the palace of Darius, but most probably
it was a specially strong part of the fortifications,
as they are there more easy of access than
elsewhere.   Outside the walls are large quarries in which are a multitude of caverns which
seem to have been appropriated to various uses ;
some having served as churches and the cells
of hermits or monks, and others as graves,
whilst some are still used as stables, and in some
cases as habitations by the poorer peasants.

The present population is mixed, the head
man being a Mohammedan Kurd, whilst the
greater number are Armenian Christians who
have a resident priest.

The head man or agha lodged us in a fine
large room and gave another for our servants,

but his hospitality did not prevent his trying
to cheat us both in the price and weight of
barley for our horses. . His houses had evidently
been largely constructed out of the ancient ruins,
and were almost the finest we came across
outside the larger towns.

All the inhabitants hunted us about with
copper coins for sale which they had dug up
in the ruins, but though we bought a good
many, they were all nearly worthless on account
of the state of decay to which they had been
reduced. Amongst the busiest and most per-
severing of the vendors, figured the priest, who
did not seem to think that his sacred calling
should prevent his turning an honest penny
when he had the chance.

CHAPTER X.

OUR road from Dara to its ancient rival
Nisibin lay across an open plain, with the
mountains to the north getting lower and more
distant, and clothed in a forest of oak scrub.

On our way we passed a village called Kasr
Serdchan, where Trotter and I got into conversation with the head man, who seemed to
be very much down on his luck. He had
some vague complaint against the authorities
at Nisibin, but was afraid to specify anything

for fear of being ill-treated if it was known
that he had reported anything to their dis-
advantage.   He said, however, that though on
the highroad · for caravans they had decreased
in numbers and wealth, and that whereas
twenty years ago they possessed twenty *chifts*,
they now only had five.   A *chift* · is a unit by
which the cultivating power of a place is
measured, and consists of a certain number of
bullocks and the instruments and men that
work with them.   In some districts the *chift*
is as high as eight bullocks and three men,
whilst in others it is as low as four and one;
here it· was between the two, each consisting
of six bullocks and two men.

In the village were the ruins of a tower
of considerable strength, which the inhabitants
said had been built by one of the sons of
the great king Darius who had built Dara.
Another son had built a castle the same distance
to the west, and as each rode to visit his father
every morning and returned in the evening, the
one who lived at Kasr Serdchan always had

the sun on his back, whilst the one who lived
to the west had it always in his eyes as he
rode to Dara and back.

Just before reaching Nisibin we were met
by the kaimacan, cadi, and other notables of
the town, who had turned out to meet the
consul. When we arrived in the town we
were taken into a poky, stuffy little room in
the cadi's house which he assured us was at
our service. Schaefer and I much preferred
our tent, and Trotter and Dr. Thom soon
thought they had better share it with us, when
we found that people were dying right and
left in the town of spotted typhus.

During the month before we arrived, one
officer, one sergeant, and eight men had died
among seventy zaptieh, and thirty men from
among the civilian population of five hundred;
no account had been taken of the women and
children. Curiously in the Christian part of the
town, which was separated from the remainder
by an open space, very few deaths had occurred.
The inhabitants had looked upon the sickness

as Kismet, and had never reported it or asked for doctors or other assistance. We heard that in the room where we had been received a man had died a couple of days before, and as it was hung with thick woollen stuffs, and the divans covered with the same, it looked as if likely to harbour infection. The illness was ascribed by the people to a stream in the mountains having changed its course and joined the Jha-Jha, which supplies the town with water.

We tried to stir up some ideas among them, and to induce them to take some sanitary precautions, which, as usual, were wofully wanting.

We soon had the melancholy satisfaction of hearing the town crier going round calling to people to bring out their dead and bury them deep, and also to bury all offal and refuse. The average death-rate was two or three a day and apparently increasing, so we were not too soon in inducing them to take some measures of precaution.

To get out of the town, we took our guns and strolled out along the branches of the

stream to see if we could get a shot, and
Schaefer got two snipe and Trotter a teal,
whilst I did not even have the satisfaction of
a miss. I could not help being amused at
the pertinacious way in which the officer of
zaptieh, whom we specially wished to avoid,
would stick to us ; the poor fellow looked very
ill himself and had nursed his brother officer
who had died only the day before.

When we got back to the tent we treated
everything to a thorough sprinkling with car-
bolic acid, and were congratulating ourselves
on being alone for the night, when a message
came from the cadi to say that he had prepared supper for us, and was coming to eat
it with us in our tent. He soon came with
a following of servants bearing trays, each with
some different article of food on it, and I must
say that he had a very good cook. When he
left us we again carbolised ourselves, and after
a prophylactic dose of quinine, turned in.

We found here that the Christians and
Mohammedans did not live very comfortably

together, and that quite lately there had been a serious dispute about a Christian woman who had been taken into a Turk's harem. The Christians were going to take her away by force, when the cadi gave orders for her to be restored peacefully. The Christians when questioned about the matter, said the cadi had behaved well on this occasion, but it was the only time in his life that he had done so.

Both Christians and Moslems had been suffering from inroads of Bedouin who had been stealing their sheep, and were reported to have carried off ten thousand belonging to Nisibin and its neighbourhood. The chief of the Tai Arabs, who are supposed to be the protectors of the Nisibin district, had come in about this matter. He was a very handsome young fellow of about eighteen, and had brought with him two hundred and fifty sheep which he asserted were all that he could find, and urged in excuse that he had only just succeeded to his father's position and found it very hard to maintain his authority.

Of the ancient glories of Nisibin, nothing, or scarcely anything, remains; a few irregular mounds show the outlines of the ramparts, but of the temples and churches which it must have contained there is not a sign. The modern town is squalid in the extreme, the most important building being a dilapidated barrack for zaptieh which was built when the Circassians were settled at Ras el Ain.

It played a most important part in ancient days, first as the frontier post of Rome, and after its supine surrender by Jovian, as that of Persia.

A fleet was once built here by Trajan, in A.D. 115, and conveyed on waggons to the upper waters of the Tigris by the Romans, in their wars against the Parthians. Here the last of the Parthian monarchs, Artabanus, defeated, after three days' fighting, the Romans under Macrinus; and this victory, the last glory of the Parthian empire, so weakened its armies, that Artaxerxes was able to success-fully carry out the revolt he had previously

planned, and which ended by establishing the
Sassanian dynasty.

In A.D. 241-42 Sapor I. captured the city
after a prolonged siege; the Persians averring
that its walls fell down in answer to their
prayers. Sapor did not long retain his conquest, for in the following year it was retaken
by the Prætorian Prefect, Timesitheus.

Nisibin by the Romans was regarded as their
principal bulwark against the hordes of the
barbarians, as they termed the Persians, and
was raised to the dignity of a colony, and most
elaborately fortified by three brick walls, and
a deep wet ditch. In its position, it could not
expect to be free from attack, and in A.D. 338
Sapor II. attacked the city. The inhabitants
vied with the garrison in their efforts to repel
the invader, and both were animated in their
defence by the prayers and example of their
bishop, St. James. A legend relates that in
answer to his prayers a plague of gnats attacked the elephants of the Persians, and
caused them in their pain and agony to trample

down and destroy many of the besieging force.
Miracles or no, after sixty-three days, Sapor
was obliged to raise the siege and retreat.

In A.D. 346, Sapor again attempted its
reduction, but after a siege of three months,
was again repulsed. The indefatigable monarch
in A.D. 348 mustered another army and advanced to its attack. The Romans advanced
to meet him, and gave him battle in the open
country near the Sinjar hills. In the day
the Romans were apparently victorious, and
when night fell gave themselves up to feasting
and revelry ; Sapor, taking advantage of their
negligence, fell upon them with troops he had
hitherto held in reserve, and the carnage was
frightful. Though ultimately successful in this
engagement, Sapor lost too many men to be
able to attack Nisibin with any prospect of
success, and he therefore retired, and did not
again attempt its capture till 350. In this
year, a civil war engaged the attention of the
Romans, and this gave Sapor the long-wished-
for opportunity. With a numerous army, and

a large number of elephants, he crossed the
Tigris, and marched on Nisibin.

The Roman governor, Count Lucilianus, was
a man of courage, genius, and resource, but the
real hero of the defence was again the brave
bishop, St. James. He strove to raise the
enthusiasm of the defendants to a level with
his own, and is said to have worked miracles
by his prayers. Sapor finding the ordinary
method of battering rams and mines unavail-
ing, tried, by damming the waters of the river—
which was then in flood, from the melting of
the snows—to surround the town by an enormous lake.   In this he is reported to have been
successful, and to have launched a fleet of
vessels carrying warlike engines, on the mimic
sea.   The townspeople still held out; but at
last Sapor thought he saw his opportunity.
The weight of the waters caused a breach in
the walls, and the attack was ordered.   The
assaulting column was composed of horse, foot,
and elephants, and advanced in an imposing
mass.   Ready to receive them stood the Roman

heavy armed troops; whilst men, women, and children laboured in the rear at the construction of a new wall. The elephants and horses of the assailants could find no secure footing, and sank in the muddy bottom of the lake; though the lighter troops were ordered to their assistance the next morning, Sapor saw, to his grief, that a new wall had already closed the gap, caused by the fall of the old one. Fortune now favoured the brave St. James and his people, for news reached Sapor that the Massagetœ were making an inroad into his own dominions, and he had to hasten back to repel these new foes, and leave Nisibin still unconquered.

In A.D. 363 the cowardly successor of the brave emperor Julian, ceded Nisibin to Sapor, as part of the price he paid for a disgraceful peace; and the Persian monarch became at length master of the much-coveted town.

In A.D. 420, the Persian general Narses took refuge in Nisibin from the Roman troops under Ardaburius, who followed him there, laid siege to the place, and came near taking it; but Varahran, unwilling to lose a place of which the value had been so well proved, marched to its succour, and forced Ardaburius to retreat. From this time until the overthrow of the Sassanian monarchy by the Arabs, Nisibin always remained in possession of the Persians.

The contour of the country round seems to render the story of the sea of Sapor rather improbable, but, no doubt, in those days what are now mere streams owing to the deforesting of the country, were then large rivers. Here we parted from Trotter and Dr. Thom, as we intended to steer straight for Mosul, across the so-called desert. We wanted some guides, and two zaptieh were told off for the duty, but seemed very loth to go; they said they did not know the way beyond a point called Tchil Agha; and when we said we would get a peasant to be guide there, said they had no money, and could not come back from Mosul without any. All these excuses were disposed of, and in the presence of the consul, they were ordered to go with us. Just as we were starting, a free fight took place between a Christian and a Mohammedan, who both used big sticks, and seemed in earnest ; friends on both sides joined in, and women and children skirmished around, flinging big stones at the combatants, though they were just as likely to hit friend as foe. After about ten minutes fighting and yelling, they all seemed to have enough, and left off apparently mutually satisfied. All this row had been about the woman who had been restored to the Christians ; either the Moslem had abused the Christian, or the Christian jeered the Moslem about the end of this case, and hot words had soon led to hard blows. I believe the Christians rather presumed on our presence, to act with greater boldness against their foes, than they would have done if the English *Balyuz* had not been there.

After bidding good-bye to Trotter and Dr. Thom, we went eastwards, whilst they steered north, towards Midyat. Our way lay across a

level fertile plain, with numerous tells, and
intersected by some small streams, whilst occasionally we saw signs of what, in exceptional
years, were devastating torrents.   Near some
of the streams, we saw some ducks, and were
lucky enough to bag half a dozen flappers,
which proved a welcome addition to our
larder.

For the first three or fours hours our zaptieh
went along in the right direction for Tchil Aga,
according to the maps, but then they began
to diverge to the north.   On asking them their
reason, they declared that they were going in
the right direction, and that the maps must
be wrong.   As several positions were rather
out, we thought perhaps they might be right,
and went on till we reached a village called
Asmaur.

We had stopped at a village just before to
ask about the road, when we were told the
zaptieh were wrong, but that at Asmaur we
should find a hospitable welcome.   The man
we spoke to said he would go on to announce

our arrival, and jumping on his mare galloped off before we had time to answer him.

As we drew near to Asmaur, we saw a number of people coming out to meet us. These were the Christian headman, and his sons, and others of the principal inhabitants. Their welcome was most effusive, as they jumped off their horses when we approached, and before we could prevent them they began kissing our boots. We dismounted and tried to prevent this, on which they went down on their knees and kissed our hands. The old chief himself at last waxed more bold, and kissed us on the shoulders; we then remounted, and rode into the village, where he put a capital house at our disposal, and prepared food for us.

When we got fairly into conversation with the old gentleman, we found that he had many complaints to make about the way the whole of the surrounding district, which was Christian, was treated by their neighbours, the Kurds. Two years ago there were twenty villages of Christians around here, now there are only ten. The people inhabiting them are Syrian Jacobites, and have no friends at court. The Kurds come down from the hills, and plunder. and destroy the property of these poor people, and then go into Nisibin and report them for making a disturbance.

The expedition against the Kurdish beys had passed by here, and lived at free quarters. for some days in the district. They were sufficiently under discipline not to personally maltreat the inhabitants, but they killed sheep and oxen, and used ploughs, and rafters of houses for firewood ; and the officers were worse than the men. When an appeal was made to the officers of the staff they laughed the suppliants to scorn, and refused to let them see the general, Izzet Pasha. They also complained a great deal of the cadi, and other authorities at Nisibin, and said that a number of ruined houses, which they pointed out, had been looted by zaptieh from Nisibin. Even whilst we were talking to the shaykh, a party of Circassians, who said they were zaptieh,

rode up, and demanded money for taxes. The
shaykh paid them, and begged us not to interfere, although they had no paper, or writing
to show their authority, and gave no receipt,
lest when we were gone, they should come
with greater numbers, and attack the village.
Whilst the Kurds who accept the Turkish
rule, plunder them with impunity, and report
them to government, they are also exposed
to the attacks of other Kurds, who are always
more or less in a state of revolt, and who say
that these poor Christians are their enemies,
because they pay taxes to the Turkish government.

Moved by the recital of the shaykh's woes,
I wrote two letters, one to Trotter, and the
other to Izzet Pasha; in the one to the latter
I appealed to the civilisation and love of justice which he was known to possess, hoping
to obtain by judicious flattery what it would
have been vain to expect by a direct demand.

From the shaykh, we learnt that our zaptieh
were taking us wrong, as I had suspected, so

we sent for them to ask their reasons. They
asserted first, that they had received private
orders from their officer not to go the way
we wished, because it was dangerous, but
round by Jezireh, which though longer, was
safer; then, that they were only ordered to go
to Tchil Agha, and return to Nisibin. Seeing
that it was no use talking to the cowardly
blackguards, I told them to go back to Nisibin,
and think themselves lucky. I did not lash them
on their horses and take them with us as
prisoners to Mosul, by the way they dreaded
so much.

A Kurd, whose ancestors had been chiefs
near here, and who still retained the title of
agha, volunteered to take us to Tchil Agha,
and also confirmed all that the shaykh had
told us, and added, that the Christians living
in fear and trembling of zaptieh and others
had sent all their flocks to the Tai Arabs, to
be taken care of, knowing that the honour of
an Arab was to be trusted, and had never
had cause to regret their confidence.

NEXT morning when we started, the shaykh
and many of his people rode out a couple of
miles with us to show us a village which had
been lately destroyed. A ruined church and
the remains of some hundred houses were at
the foot of a mound, by which flowed a stream
called the Nahr al Fieruz or the Turquoise
stream. This village until within a year had been
inhabited, and the church had been the centre
of the Christian life of the surrounding district.

Here we said good-bye to our host, and

rode on with the agha. Our road was across an open and almost level country, only slightly broken, where a few streams flowed through a tract where granite cropped up through the calcareous limestone which formed the usual surface of the country.

Just beyond this was a Tel, on the summit of which was perched the stronghold of a Kurdish agha, Muran by name, chief of the village of Mask'ouk, which lay scattered at the foot of the mound. Our guide took us up here, and Muran gave us coffee, and wanted us to interest ourselves on his behalf as he said he was badly treated by the government, and especially by the cadi of Nisibin. Poor cadi, every one seemed to think they had a right to abuse him. Our guide told us, as we rode away, that he had taken us up to Muran agha's hold in order that we should see a specimen of a real old Kurd, who only acknowledged the authority of the Turkish government when he thought fit to do so, and whose only real complaint was that, when his business

called him into Nisibin, he found it best to
have a fat present in his hand in order to
induce the cadi to overlook the robberies he
had committed. He said Muran had plundered
many of the Christian villages of which we
had been told the night before, and was the
greatest bandit in the country.

We reached Tchil Agha about four in the
afternoon, and tried to get a guide for Mosul ;
after some bargaining two men promised to
go with us for a hundred piastres. In the
morning both had thought better of it ; and
though others volunteered, the manner of payment was a difficulty ; the people had never
seen a gold coin and would not look at one,
and as our stock of change was running short
we were puzzled what to do. In this dilemma
a man who had joined himself on to our party
to go to Mosul, proved of use, for he had
stowed away in his saddle a goodly stock of
medjidies which, when he heard of our dilemma,
he brought out. We had at first agreed to
pay half in advance, but when the guide saw

the money he wanted the whole at once. He then proposed to us to give the money to the head man who was to return it if he failed in his task, whilst he swore by heaven and by hell, by father and by mother, by wife and by children, that he would not desert us, but would go straight on with us to Mosul.

When all these preliminaries were settled we rode away eastward, until soon after noon we sighted a mound near which were grazing innumerable flocks of sheep and goats tended by Kurdish shepherds. Scattered camps were dotted along the banks of a stream, and near them strayed the horses and camels of their owners.

This was Rumeilat, a great grazing-place of the Kurds at this time of the year, and the stream was the easternmost affluent of the Khabour and therefore of the Euphrates. Here we were to halt to water our animals, as the next place where we should be able to do so was ten or twelve hours distant. We off packed and made a fire, whilst the shepherds

crowded round to stare at us; we asked them
if they could get some milk, and instead of, like
Arabs, bringing it as a present, they wanted
to be shown the money before they would take
the trouble of going to their tents to fetch
any. They were fine wild-looking fellows, and
their dress was picturesque and serviceable. It
consisted of a coloured calico shirt and gaily
striped loose trousers of the same stuff; over
the shirt they wore a jumper of stiff felt about
an inch thick, of which the angles at the
shoulders stood out prominently, with a hood
hanging down behind. This jumper, when
they squat on the ground and pull the hood
over their heads, shelters them from any storm.
On their heads they wore conical felt caps
nearly as high as that of Bahri Bey, with
handkerchiefs coiled round the base.

They live in a constant state of skirmish and
warfare with the neighbouring Arabs, of whom
the Shammar and Tai were said lately to have
carried off five flocks, each consisting of from
250 to 300 sheep from this very place.

Early in the afternoon we started again,
and some four miles from the stream met an
old man hurrying in with his flocks, who
told us he had seen forty Arabs ride by just
before, and that we were sure to be robbed
and murdered. Thanking him for his kindly
caution we rode on without paying much
attention to it.

At sunset we passed some ancient earthworks
which looked very much like a Roman camp,
and a poor stray sheep dog joined us. Poor
fellow, he had lost his masters, and was almost
starved. Two hours later we camped for the
night, and slept out under the blue sky. We
had taken the precaution to fill our air pillows
with water, which supplied enough for the men,
dogs, and horses; the muleteers did not seem to
care about the animals going thirsty, and indeed had complained of the extra weight of the
little water we did carry. The poor stray dog
was so thirsty that it was unable to eat until
it had drunk, and then it showed what an
appetite it had. We were soon all asleep with

the exception of a man keeping guard, and as
the men were in a great fright at being out in
the desert, without even a tent being pitched,
we could trust to a good look out being
kept.

At half-past three in the morning I woke
up, and looked at one of the watches and saw
it showed half-past five, but I quite forgot that
it was two hours fast. I roused up the people
and hurried on the start, and we got away
quickly. As we rode along in the dark, I
could not make out why the day did not dawn,
and until I struck a light and again looked at
the watch, when I found it showed seven
o'clock, and that there was not the least sign
of day-break in the east, I did not discover
my mistake. The sun did rise at last, and
right glad we were to welcome his warming
rays, as there had been a sharpish frost, and
riding along at a foot pace in the dark was not
agreeable.

We passed some more mounds which seemed
to be man's handiwork, and to have formed at

one time the defences of an entrenched camp ; and at about nine o'clock we sighted black tents on both sides of our path, and soon after came to a lot of pools of fresh water lying in the bed of a stream.

Here we halted for breakfast, and Schaefer and I went after some duck and teal, which were plentiful ; we bagged a few ; Schaefer making one most extraordinary right and left shot : the second teal must have been at least seventy yards off when killed.

Kurds, from the camps near, coming down with donkeys to fetch water, frightened our timid followers very much. I was lying down enjoying a pipe, and basking in the sun, after we had finished breakfast, when the silly old cry of *Arrahmy ! Arrahmy !!* was raised ; and when I refused to get up, all our men began to swear that an unlimited number of Kurdish or Arab robbers were coming, and that they must run away. I soon stopped their running, and looking at the supposed robbers, found that three men and two women had caused all this alarm amongst our eight or, counting the guide, nine followers.

We resumed our march at one o'clock, and soon afterwards commenced crossing small spurs of the Sinjar mountains, which ran down into the plain we had been traversing, and which stretched away to the Tigris, a little north of Mosul. The poor dog we had picked up the day before would not leave the water; perhaps the memory of the thirst he had undergone was more vivid than that of hunger. As there were camps near we hoped that he might soon find new masters, and we left some food for him, so that, at all events for one day, he should not suffer from want of victuals.

Amongst the spurs of the hills, were several gazelle scattered about in parties of four or five. As it was no use attempting to course them with greyhounds, I tried patient stalking; several times just as I was getting within range the noise of the muleteers would startle my intended prey; but at last my perseverance was rewarded, and I got within a hundred and fifty yards of three, and carefully selecting the biggest, sent a Henry expanding bullet into his *pot pourri.* He went a short distance, but another through his heart dropped him dead.

As we went along, we began to get into traces of former villages, and flocks and camps became more numerous, whilst streams from the hills flowed away towards the Tigris, whose basin we had at last reached. The largest sort of bustards were common, but shy, and though I suppose I walked seven or eight miles trying to get a shot at them, I never succeeded in getting within range. Creeping up a watercourse, or behind the crest of a hill was no use; when we arrived at the point where, according to the birds' former position, they would be within range, it would be only to find that the provoking creatures had flown away, and settled down again some seven or eight hundred yards further off. Once I made sure that I should be able to get within shot, as the cock bird was strutting

and drumming in the middle of four hens who
seemed lost in admiration of their lord's performance.   One, however, was not so wrapt
in admiration as to be unable to see me
coming, and she gave the alarm, when the
cock bird, attended by his harem, took flight.

At sunset we camped near a stream; but as
we intended to start early the next morning,
so as to reach Mosul, if possible, the same
day, we did not pitch our tents, but slept "*à
l'auberge de la belle étoile.*"   Schaefer's last
words to me before we went to sleep were,
"*N'oubliez point que la montre est trop
avancée par deux heures.*"

There was no need to remind me of this,
for I never opened my eyes till the sun rose,
being tired after the long day and the amount
of walking I had done.

We were soon on the road, and at half-past
eight we passed a place called Hogna, where
there was a large building surrounded by a
loop-holed wall, which was said to be a sort
of barrack for zaptieh from Mosul, when they

came out to collect taxes from the Kurds. A ruined building, apparently some hundreds of years old, stood close by; and there was a permanent camp of Kurds, who cultivated a little ground—the first cultivation we had seen since leaving Tchil Agha.

A short way beyond Hogna, we passed the remains of an ancient canal; and thenceforward our way lay through country of which a fair proportion was cultivated, though villages were few and far between. Our guide was now rather out in his knowledge of the country, or perhaps was afraid of going into Mosul; and at sunset, we found ourselves near a half ruined village on the banks of the Tigris, some distance to the north of the town. Here we found encamped a party in charge of sixty or seventy horses, which belonged to inhabitants of Mosul, and which they were taking about the country in search of pasture. They were very anxious to know the prospects of food and water in the tract we had come through, as, owing to the winter rains having been very scanty, the country was suffering from drought.

Next morning, our guide said that he had now brought us close to Mosul, and that he hoped we would allow him to leave us as many enemies of his tribe lived there; permission was readily granted, and he went away delighted with a small extra present.

Schaefer and I rode on with Gabriel, leaving the mules to follow; and following a well worn track, we arrived at the gates of Mosul in about an hour and a half. The zaptieh on guard at the gate seemed inclined to dispute our entrance, but we rode straight in, and explaining who we were, got one of them to show the way to the English consulate. Just inside the walls was a large open space with only a few ruined houses in it, this was the part of the town that suffered most severely when the plague last visited Mosul. Crossing this, we got into the usual narrow winding streets of an Eastern town, and soon reached the consulate, where we rather astonished Mrs.

Russell by our arrival, as a rumour had reached Mosul that we had given up all idea of going there. Her husband, the vice-consul, a son of Dr. W. H. Russell, was out shooting; but she made us at home at once, and sent a message to tell him we had arrived.

The bright, home-like appearance of Mrs. Russell's home, with pet birds, and dogs running in and out of the rooms, and gazelle in the courtyard; book-cases full of well read volumes; a work table, and other signs of an English lady's presence in this out-of-the-way place, was indeed refreshing after having been so long without seeing anything of the sort.

Russell himself came in as soon as he heard of our arrival, and both he and his wife vied in their efforts to make us feel comfortable and at home. He was in some sort a fellow African, having been twice up to Khartoum, and once to Gondokoro, on Gordon Pasha's staff, but had been compelled to relinquish his appointment on account of bad health.

Our first question was as to how to make
our way to Baghdad; and as we intended
following the right bank of the Tigris, it was
necessary to make arrangements with the
Arabs, who command all the country on that
side of the river.

As luck would have it, Ferhan Pasha, the
shaykh of the Shammar, was in Mosul, where
he had come to make arrangements about re-
capturing some sheep belonging to the people
of Mosul, which had been carried off by the
Aneyzeh Arabs ; and so a message was sent
off to him to tell him of our intention, and to
ask him to arrange that we should not be
molested. An answer soon came that all
would be right ; and that he was sorry he
could not come to see us as he was going
to leave Mosul early next morning.

Ferhan Pasha is paid by the Turkish
Government three thousand pounds a year to
protect the flocks of the Mosulotes from raids
by other Arab tribes ; and lately the Aneyzeh
had made a successful raid and driven off

about fifty thousand sheep.   One of Ferhan's
sons had recaptured a small number, but the
remainder had been carried too far away for
Ferhan's people to pursue them without assistance, and Ferhan was asking for two tabors
of infantry to help him.   He said that he also
had lost many sheep by the raid, and that
the fair way of arranging matters would be
. that those recovered by the Shammar should
be kept by them, and that the troops should
take to Mosul any they might get.   Naturally
the governor of Mosul said that Ferhan being
paid to protect the flocks belonging to the
town, he should first return them, and then
look after his own ; to which Ferhan replied
that before the agreement was entered into
the townspeople did not dare to pasture any
sheep to the west of the Tigris, and that now
they had over a million feeding there.   I afterwards heard that, in the end, Ferhan never
got any back from the true Aneyzeh, being
afraid to come into collision with them, but
made a raid on semi-nomad Arabs belonging

to the vilayet of Aleppo, and took their flocks
to replace those carried off.

Of course one of the first things to be done
at Mosul was to cross the river and see the
excavations at Koyunjik, the site of the ancient
Nineveh. Although the excavations are still
being carried on, there was very little to be
seen ; and a visit to the British Museum would
give a far better idea of the glories of ancient
Nineveh than a passing visit to the mounds
which hide its ruins. It is much to be regretted
that the bigotry of the Mohammedans prevent
excavations being made in the mound on which
is the supposed tomb of the prophet Jonah,
as there no doubt would be found remains
of equal interest and importance with those
that have rewarded the labours of Sir Henry
Layard and his successors in the other
mounds.

Schaefer unfortunately was unwell, having
caught cold during our journey from Nisibin, so
having completed letter writing, I got Russell
to ask Unis Bey, a rich Turk, to give us a

day with his hawks, being very anxious to see the ancient sport of hawking.

Unis Bey responded by inviting us to accompany him and bring our greyhounds. We found him accompanied by a party of about twenty, eight of whom carried hawks, whilst six led greyhounds. The first part was for coursing, and we went down on to the plains bordering the river just above the town, crossing on the way sulphur springs smelling like rotten eggs; on the face. of the small cliffs which divide the plain from the upper country were outcrops of marble, no doubt formed by the same volcanic agency to which the springs can be attributed.

Once on the plain we soon found a hare, and though all nine dogs were after her she gave a very good run. Nimshi, after the first couple of minutes, was the only one that kept her in view, but the unfortunate hare in doubling to escape her, ran right across the other greyhounds which were headed by Richan and Saada, one of whom chopped her.

Ten minutes afterwards we turned up another
hare, and after a long and exciting chase she
ran to earth, our three greyhounds again being
to the front, Unis Bey's being, like their master,
too fat for work.

Unis Bey now declared that the dogs were
tired, and we rode on to an island in the
river which was covered with brush and small
trees, and which was said to be full of francolin.
We formed into a line so as to drive along
this, and soon had several françolin on the
wing, at which the hawks were loosed. Instead
of soaring up and making a swoop at their
quarry, the hawks flew straight after them
(technically called raking, I believe) and captured them by their superior speed. This did
not prove very interesting, as the francolin flew
low among the trees in their efforts to escape
their pursuer, and little or nothing could be
seen of the way they were caught. Russell
and I therefore took our guns, and amused
ourselves by shooting pigeon, of which there
were an enormous quantity, and soon made

a good bag of them. Whilst we were shooting pigeons I heard an alarm of pig, and
Russell fire a rifle; I went to him, and he
said he had seen a sounder of pig, and fired
at a boar, but they had gone clean away; so
I left him and went down to the bank of the
river to try for some duck. Suddenly I heard
shouts of Khansir! Khansir!! (Boar! Boar!!)
and looking round, saw all Unis Bey's people
making for their horses, and in a great per-
turbation. I changed my shot cartridges for
ball, and going to where the boar was supposed
to be, I saw his crest just appearing above
some brush at the foot of a tree. I was then
about twenty yards from him, and so, taking
a careful aim for where I supposed his heart
to be, fired. He got up on his legs and
attempted to come at me, but a bullet through
the head ended his earthly career before he
had traversed half the distance. On looking
at him I found that he had been wounded
before, and was, no doubt, the same one that
Russell had fired at. He had been so hard

hit by Russell's shot that he would have been dead in another ten minutes without my intervention, so, according to the laws of *venerie*, he was Russell's pig. After this we went on looking for more pig, but though we saw several on the move could not get within range. Whilst looking for pig I was within an ace of shooting a yearling black bull. In the brush I saw a black mass and thought it was a wild boar, and took aim ; just as I was going to press the trigger I saw the beast move, and, much to my disgust, a horned head appear out of the scrub.

When we returned into the town we found our bag was, one hare killed by the greyhounds, and twenty-one francolin by the hawks, whilst the joint bag of Russell and myself was one wild boar, thirty-seven pigeons, five francolin, one plover, six snipe and two teal—not a bad mixed bag.

For all information respecting Nineveh I cannot do better than refer the reader to the works of Sir Henry Layard. The modern

town of Mosul has been of importance since
the days of the Mohammedan conquest; the
ruins called Eski Mosul, a few miles further
up the river, mark the site of an older town
of the same name, which is the one that was
known to the Romans.

The present importance of the town lies in
its being the great point for crossing the Tigris
by the caravans from Baghdad who prefer the
circuitous route by Erbil and Kerkuk with its
many difficulties, to running the risk of being
attacked by the Bedouins.   A rickety bridge of
boats connects the eastern and western banks
of the river, and on the low land on the eastern
side which is covered when the river is in flood
is an arched causeway, so that, when owing to
bad weather or other causes the boats are
removed, it seems as if the bridge had been
built on dry land instead of across the river.

The most important missionary and educational establishment is that of the Dominican
fathers.   The whole force consists of a Papal
delegate, six or seven fathers, and twelve sisters.

They have native teachers to assist them, and their scholars number between four and five hundred. They have a large congregation, and have built a large and handsome church besides a small chapel in an orphanage conducted by the sisters. They minister to bodily as well as spiritual and intellectual wants, and every day relief is administered to between a hundred and fifty and two hundred people, irrespective of sect or religion.

The Chaldeans who are very numerous here are not so prosperous, and are split up into two bodies, one of which has accepted the authority of the Pope whilst the other claims independence. These are severally known as the "wet" and "dry" Chaldeans, or the bullites and anti-bullites. Some time ago a dispute arose as to which of the two divisions the four Chaldean churches at Mosul should belong, and the Porte said that each were to have two. This did not give satisfaction, as the different sites were supposed to be of different degrees of sanctity; so at last the Turks, being wearied of the disputes, settled the matter by building a wall in each church that divided it into two halves longitudinally, and each sect was given a half of each church.

CHAPTER XII.

ALTHOUGH Ferhan Pasha had left without
seeing us, he had arranged with the governor
for us to have an Arab escort as far as
Samara, so as to avoid all difficulties with
any wandering Bedouins that we might meet
on the way. Accordingly, one day, there was
ushered into Mrs. Russell's drawing-room, an

Arab shaykh in all the glories of a new abba, or cloak, red morocco boots, and gorgeous head-dress. This was Shaykh Mohammed, chief of the Abou Hamed tribe of Arabs, who are feudatories of the Shammar. The shaykh himself, as well as his lord, was paid a sum of money every year both to abstain from robbing himself and prevent others from doing so.

He announced that he himself was going with us, and would take half a dozen of his tribe, who should meet us at Hammam Ali, some four hours south of Mosul.

We arranged with him that we should start the next day, and despatched our mules and servants at daybreak. Soon after they had started it came on to rain heavily, and when the shaykh arrived he proposed that we should wait till the rain stopped. We waited and waited, but the rain instead of getting less, got heavier and heavier, until at last we gave up all hopes of any amendment, and started.

A more unpleasant ride it was scarcely possible to imagine, the rain finding its way into every crack and cranny in spite of waterproofs, and running down into one's boots until they were actually full. The first part of the road lay along a perfect level, across which we went as fast as we could, though at the imminent danger of the horses falling from the slipperiness of the mud, but we had after five miles to go through hills for a couple of miles, and any other horses than Arabs would have been puzzled to get up and down the slippery muddy banks of small streams, and along the track which the shaykh showed us as a short cut. Soon after passing through these hills we came to a wretched, dirty village, where we found our people halted, the muleteers having refused to go on any further in the rain, though Hammam Ali, where we were to meet our other Arabs, was only three miles off.

Nothing had been done to get any place ready for us, the rain seemed to have washed all the small wits out of our servants' heads. Our led horses were standing out in the rain, and the baggage all lying in a muddy swamp, although our people had been in the village some four hours. The only man who had any remains of wits was Elias the cook, who had his fire lit and some coffee ready.

We soon found stabling for the horses, and shelter, such as it was, for ourselves, though the rain dripping through the sooty and leaky roof seemed to bid fair to convert us all into the likeness of Christy Minstrels. We, however, managed to rig up an awning under the roof so as to keep the drips off a space large enough for our sleeping bags, and got inside them as the most comfortable place to spend the evening in.

Next morning we found it had stopped raining, but our shaykh when he appeared was a very different-looking object from the gorgeous apparition he had been in Mrs. Russell's drawing-room; not only had the thorough soaking of the day before caused

all the brightness of his colours to be spoilt,
but he was also all spotted with black from
water that had been dripping on him during
the night; and he said he could go no further
than Hammam Ali, as he wanted to take a
bath there after his ducking.

We rode across a level plain to the sulphur
spring which gives its name to the place,
and which was covered over by a ruinous
building. We looked inside, and saw some
people disporting themselves in what looked
like dirty dish water with pieces of grease
and soot floating on the surface, whilst the
nostrils were assailed by the scent of rotten
eggs. The temperature of the water was
130°; and in the spring a large portion of the
population of Mosul come and camp out here,
in order to avail themselves of these baths
which are said to have medicinal qualities,
and to be especially efficacious in rheumatism
and skin diseases. Notwithstanding its healing
virtues we did not make use of the spring,
but preferred our baths in our tent, and to

use the water of the Tigris, instead of its
medicinal produce.

The shaykh and all his people, together
with our muleteers and servants, took advantage
of the bath; and in the course of the afternoon our curiosity was excited by seeing
a kelluk, or raft of skins, floating down
the river, with a man in European clothes
standing by a cabin built on its surface. As
the kelluk touched the bank we showed our
colours, in the hopes that it might bear some
European traveller, but the person who excited
our curiosity proved to be the Persian consul
at Mosul, who was on his way to Baghdad, and
who had stopped here to bathe.

Opposite our camp was the great mound of
Nimroud, the site of Calah, the second city of
the Assyrian empire. Sir Henry Layard made
here the discovery of the "black obelisk," perhaps the most important of all the records of the
Assyrian monarchy; and excavations were still
going on under the direction of Mr. Rassam
when we passed by.

The next morning we got away early, the shaykh promising that we should make good marches and reach Sherghat, Ferhan Pasha's head-quarters, the next day. The escort now consisted of the shaykh himself,- one of his sons, four other Arabs, and a negro, who was the old man's servant. One of the rank and file was a Shammar who had left his own tribe in consequence of some trouble, and attached himself to the shaykh. This fellow now professed himself to be devoted to us, and said that he was our servant, and would go anywhere and do anything for us. Like most large talkers, he was a bad performer; and we afterwards found, that he made use of his position to cheat both us and the inhabitants of the country.

We marched for eight hours and a half across a fairly level country, the only break being at the beginning and ending of the day's march, when we changed from the lower alluvial plain bordering the river, to the more elevated great southern plain of Mesopotamia.

The change was made by easy slopes, and
would offer no difficulty to the engineer, unless
he preferred to keep altogether on the higher
level.

Nothing worthy of remark during the whole
day, except an ancient canal about thirty feet
wide.   In the evening we halted at the tents
of Shaykh Azowy, one of the sub-chiefs of the
Abou Hamed Arabs, close to the river's bank.
Here we were warmly welcomed, and sheep
and fowls were killed in our honour, and we
had to eat with the two shaykhs, and the son
of Shaykh Mohammed—all the other Arabs
waiting till we had finished.

Our path the next morning took us past
sulphur springs and bitumen ponds, after which
we kept along the lower plain. A few scrubby
oaks and prickly shrubs of acacia were all the
vegetation, except grass, which we met with.
Several small parties of Jebour Arabs were
moving about, with their belongings packed on
donkeys.   Kids and lambs too young to walk
were stuffed into bags, and slung across the

loads, with their poor little heads hanging out,
and swinging about at every step of the donkeys. They kept up a most piteous bleating,
in which they were joined by their anxious
mammas who trotted along close by.

About noon we started a fox, and had a
capital run with the greyhounds; although the
dogs were much faster than the fox the latter
was so cunning in doubling and twisting, that
it almost made good its escape into some
rough and broken ground, where it would
have been safe; but the fates were against it,
and an unfortunate double gave Nimshi a
chance which she was not slow in availing
herself of. Though nearly disabled by the
first grip, the fox fought gamely, and inflicted
two or three bites, though none were serious,
on his captors. The shaykh asked for the
skin, as it would be useful for lining a winter
cloak, so the carcase was given to his servant
to flay.

Soon after this we came upon a quantity of
cultivation most cunningly irrigated by a

series of small ditches which seemed more complicated than any labyrinth. The water which supplied this system was raised from rivers in skins which were hauled up by bullocks, as is shown in the sketch. The face

BULLOCK RAISING WATER.

of the river bank was revetted with faggots of brushwood, and the trench into which the water fell from the skins was also filled with brushwood, in order to prevent the wash and splash doing any damage.

Just beyond this cultivated ground was a
camp of Jebour Arabs, situated in the midst of
a tangled brake of brushwood. · These Jebours
are Arabs who cultivate the ground, and in consequence are much despised by their nomad
brethren. Those we met here were feudatory to
Ferhan Pasha, and said that they were Shammar
Arabs, but the real Shammar repudiate their
claim with scorn.

Most of the people lived in tents, but some
of the poorer ones had holes dug in the ground
in which they slept and kept their scanty belongings. I asked the chief the reason why
he and his people lived in the sort of jungle
in which their camp was made, and he said
that it formed an efficient defence against the
Bedouins of the plains who sometimes tried
to drive off their cattle and sheep, but were
always easily baffled by turning the flocks into
the brushwood.

The chief gave a sheep to our escort and
servants, and sent us a lamb for ourselves ; the
latter our cook managed to roast whole, and we

invited the chief and our shaykh to join us at dinner, but the Jebour did not care to come to meet his superior.

After the shaykh had left us however, the Jebour chief came to see us and to prefer a petition; he said that he and a brother were now joint shaykhs over a branch of the Jebour tribe, but that his brother was a sickly useless sort of fellow, and therefore it would be much better if all the power were lodged in his own hands. He promised if, by our intercession with Ferhan Pasha we could arrange this little business for him, his two best mares should be at our disposal.

During the night there was a very heavy thunderstorm, accompanied by sharp squalls of wind and torrents of rain. We feared for the safety of our tent, but it held out bravely. Our servants were not so fortunate and the unfortunate Arabs who lived in holes were fairly flooded out of them. When the day broke they were to be seen wet and shivering, fishing their belongings out of the pools which,

over night, had been dry and warm dwelling
places.

Four hours' march brought us to Sherghat,
the headquarters of Ferhan Pasha, all the
road being level except for about half a mile,
where we had to cross a sort of promontory
running out on to the lower plain close by the
Wady Meksir.

Ferhan himself and most of his sons and
people were away about the sheep stolen from
the Mosulotes, but two sons, the elder about
fourteen, were in the camp, and did their best
to welcome us. We had to have supper with
them in their large tent, and I was rather glad
that it took place in comparative darkness, as
the glimpses one got of the contents of the
huge platter which contained the food when
the fire occasionally blazed up, were not inviting.
A sheep had been hacked to pieces by some one
totally ignorant of anatomy, and then boiled,
and afterwards a sort of sweet grease made of
fat, milk, and sugar had been poured over it.
The cooking had not been more careful than

the cutting up, and in addition to splinters of·
bone, one often found foreign ‚matters such as
grit and ashes in one's mouth, whilst a decided
flavour of smoke pervaded the whole.   When
this ordeal was over coffee and pipes were produced—and coffee, as it is only to be found in an
Arab's tent, makes up for many shortcomings.

The people all begged for powder for their
matchlocks as they said they had very little,
and that very bad.   Their guns being long and
badly balanced, many had fixed a pair of legs
with spiked ends on to the fore end of the
barrels.   These were covered with the skin
of the legs of gazelle shrunk on to strengthen
them, and hinged to the barrel so as to lie
alongside it when not in use.   With immense
patience and caution they stalk both birds and
beasts, and when near, plant their support in
the ground so that they are able to take a
very steady pot shot.   It often happens, as
might be expected, that whilst the process of
pivoting the gun is proceeding, the intended
prey departs and another stalk has to be under-

taken. When flocks of birds are feeding they will direct their weapon towards their midst and fire when some unlucky one crosses the line of sight. In this way, a boy of ten years old killed two francolin at one shot with a·bullet whilst we were looking on.

Sherghat was explored by Sir Henry Layard when engaged in his work of searching for the antiquities of these regions, and he was well rewarded for his labours. Now, nothing is to be seen except a few holes or caves, and the mounds which cover the ancient city. It is supposed to have been the Asshur of the Chaldeans; and Shamas-Vul, son of Ismi-Dagon, who reigned *circa* 1850 B.C., built a temple here to the gods Ana and Vul.

In 1300 B.C. Asshur was the seat of the Assyrian monarchy, which was just assuming its importance, the towns of Nineveh and Nimrud not being then in existence. A cylinder found here has been translated by Sir Henry Rawlinson, and gives us the history and genealogy of the great King Tiglath

Pileser I. Now, instead of a city the capital
of an empire, only a few tents of semi-nomad
Arabs are to be seen.

Leaving Sherghat we gradually ascended on
to the higher plain, having the commencement
of the Hamrin mountains between us and the
river though here only about a hundred and
fifty feet higher than the plain. About noon we
met a party of Abou Hamed Arabs who were
wandering about with their camels and flocks,
and Shaykh Mohammed and his son dismounted
to talk to them; once they began to yarn there
was no moving them, and after we had wasted
over an hour it was discovered that it was time
to camp. We moved on a short way to where
a wady broke through the hills towards the
river. In this wady, in order to be sheltered
from wind and hostile observation, the camp
was formed. The bottom of the wady was proposed to us as being the best place to camp,
but I was too old a traveller to pitch our tent
there in unsettled weather. The Arabs thought
differently, and their tents were pitched as low

down as possible, some in the very sole of the valley.

All the work of unloading the camels, pitching the tents, collecting brushwood for fires and cooking fell to the share of the women, the lordly sons of the desert not condescending, to more menial work than making coffee. The camels were made to kneel down and have their loads taken off, the great black sheets of camels and goats' hair spread out, pegs driven in, ropes and stays made fast, poles raised and cushions spread by the gentler sex, who then informed their lords and masters that all was ready for their accommodation.

This place was called by the Arabs Bel-a-dij, and was a favourite camping place, and in ordinary years would have been occupied long before this, but the lateness and scarcity of the rainfall had caused it to be left unoccupied until now.

In the early part of the night we were much disturbed by wolves and jackals; a wolf indeed made its way right into the midst of one of the flocks, but was driven away with shouts and firebrands before it had done any serious damage. When the wild animals became quiet, thunder and rain commenced, with blinding lightning, and heavy squalls. Our precaution of camping on the higher level had been a good one, for soon the bottom of the wady was a rushing torrent, and two or three of the Arabs' tents were washed away, whilst others were flooded, and some lambs and kids carried away by the rushing waters were drowned. The shouts and curses of men and women, the barking of dogs, and bleating of sheep and goats, mingled with the wind and formed a sort of infernal charivari. Though we were better off than our friends and neighbours, we still could not afford to be passive lookers-on, as our mules got frightened and stampeded, tearing up their pickets from the moistened ground, and every moment the squalls striking against our tent, each one seeming heavier than the last, threatened to carry it away bodily. No sooner was one peg driven home than another drew, and some of us had to hold on to the tent ropes, whilst others searched for stones to pile on the pegs and thus strive to keep them in their places. After over an hour's struggle with the elements the storm began to abate, and by two in the morning the stars were shining peacefully in a clear blue sky, and not a cloud was to be seen. We found our mules all huddled together in a small ravine about half a mile away, and by three o'clock, as far as we were concerned, matters were arranged as comfortably as could be expected; but the poor devils of Arabs were all wet and shivering : their bedding had been drenched, their stock of firewood had been washed away, and it was too dark to look for more. We luckily had some charcoal, and lit a fire and made coffee for all who came to beg for it, whilst one or two came slinking into our tent to ask if we could not spare them a little brandy.

When we left in the morning the lost property had mostly been found, the flocks

counted, and the tents were being shifted up
to the same level where ours had been pitched,
the Arabs at last admitting that we had been
wiser than they.

Leaving the camp we were an hour crossing
a confused congeries of wadys, all of which
showed traces of the last night's storm, and
then we came upon a plain bounded to the
east by the Hamrin Mountains, and stretching
to the south and west further than the eye
could reach. Scattered about this plain were
little camps of two or three tents each, but we
soon passed all these, and our Arabs began to
show signs of uneasiness about their night's
lodging. The next camp of which they were
sure was too far distant to be reached the
same day, and the shaykh sent his men up -
into the mountains to see if they could find
a place where we might halt. We soon saw
a small flock, and riding towards it, the shepherd told us that there were two or three
tents just behind a spur of the hills. Shaykh
Mohammed declared that we must halt there,

and, though much disappointed by the short-
ness of the march, we agreed to let him do so.

Arriving at the tents we found a man just
going out after some mountain sheep, of which
a herd had been seen by some women collecting fuel. I changed my boots, and started off
with him for where they had been seen, but
when we arrived they had all gone away;
the man wanted to go back, but I persuaded
him to go on, and after about another hour's
walking and climbing we saw one on the
opposite side of a ravine, but clean out of
range; it was a solitary female, and feeding.
I found that by going round the head of the
ravine, I should be able to approach her up
wind and under shelter of some rocks. I
crept round very cautiously, but do what I
would I could not avoid my boots making
a noise on the stones, and when at two hundred
and fifty yards from her I saw her lift her head
and listen. I kept as quiet as possible, and
squatting down behind a rock took off my
boots, and belt with knife and pistol, and then

crawled along towards her. She was evidently
very suspicious, and moved two or three times,
but at last I got within easy range. I don't
know what came over me, but I got so nervous
that I couldn't hold my rifle steady. I raised
it to my shoulder two or three times and had
to put it down again. She then moved again,
and suddenly I became as steady as a rock,
and, drawing a steady bead, rolled her over
dead. As the smoke cleared away I saw the
remainder of the herd—which had been nearer
than her, but hidden by some rocks, bounding
away up the mountain-side. I slipped in a
fresh cartridge and took a flying shot, but it
was no use; and the patriarch of the herd with
heavy horns and beard took his flock away
in safety. By the time I had got my boots
on again I could see them miles away on the
summit of the hills, and it was useless to go
after them, so I left the carcase under the
care of the man who had followed me, and
went back to camp to send some one to help
him to bring it in.

When the carcase arrived in camp the wretches had cut off the feet, and so generally mutilated it that any measurements or accurate description was out of the question. It was roughly about the size of an ordinary sheep, with short, thick, coarse dark reddish-brown hair, underlaid by a soft wool of the same colour, and had straight horns two inches in length. I found the horn of a male in one of the tents, which was recurved, flattened, and nodose, its measurements were—exterior curve, thirty inches; interior, nineteen and a half inches; and circumference at base, nine and seven-eighths inches. The beard of the male I saw on the mountain seemed to extend along the lower part of the throat and chest between the forelegs, like the sheep of Manyuema, and the aoudad of Abyssinia and Barbary.

When we left this camp we marched for twenty miles along the plain, which was perfectly level, and only broken by occasional watercourses; Sultan, whom I was riding, was in very great spirits, and I indulged him in some gallops much to his delight; in one of which we came suddenly upon one of these gullies, and if he had not jumped pluckily, we should have come to grief; as it was we cleared it in safety. When I rode back to see what it was like, I found it about fifteen feet wide, and six deep—not a bad leap for an Arab horse, who had scarcely ever jumped in his life, to clear.

During the day we had a succession of cold rain squalls from the north, though in the intervals the sun shone bright and warm. At the commencement of one of these the thermometer marked 84° Fahr., and after it had continued ten minutes, 56°.

At the end of the plain we came upon a salt stream working its way through some low sand hills towards the Tigris, which had just broken through the Hamrin Hills; and five miles further on we came to a camp of Jebour Arabs, situated amongst the brushwood on a branch of the river. Close by were the ruins of an ancient castle called by· the Arabs Kala'-at Mekrun, which seemed to be of Roman architecture. Curiously enough, the position was wrong in latitude though right in longitude, and this is not the only instance of positions being wrong in latitude in the places on the banks of the Tigris.

Here we for the first time came upon humped cattle like the Indian ones; and had to feed our horses on gram instead of on barley.

Eight hours the next day took us to Tekrit, the road for the first half of the distance lying along the low land near the river, and then rising up about seventy feet on to the higher level. We met many small parties marching northwards, some of them were men who had taken goods down to Baghdad on kelluks, and were now returning with the skins packed on donkeys, others were seeking for pasture for sheep, and others were bands of sturdy

pilgrims returning from some of the sacred
places in southern Mesopotamia, and who
seemed to think that the religious purpose
of their journey gave them a right to demand
alms from all they met.

TEKRIT, at present a " very abomination of
desolation," was anciently a place of considerable
importance, and commanded one of the ferries
across the Tigris.   It resisted successfully the
victorious armies of Sapor, and was always considered as impregnable until it was taken, after
a stubborn resistance, by Tamerlane.   Notwithstanding its supposed impregnability it was sur-
rendered to the Moslems in the year 637, after

Khosru-sum, the general of Isdigerd, had been defeated at Kasr-i-Shirin by El Kakaa, the Arab commander. It is supposed that Tekrit is the place where the retreating Romans under Jovian recrossed the Tigris after the death of the ill-starred Julian.

The place now consists of a quantity of confused ruins, and a few mean houses built of Roman bricks. When we came into the town we at first vainly looked for a place where we might pitch our tents, and when at last we selected one near the river bank, a zaptieh came from the mudir and said that he had orders not to permit us to camp there. We sent for the mudir, and showing our firman asked what he meant by his impertinent message. He would not give any reason, and then began to beg for money. I ordered the tents to be pitched, and told him that unless he behaved more civilly I should report him at Baghdad. He then declared it was all a mistake, and that the zaptieh had been sent to show us a better place. Failing to get money out of us, the

mudir wanted raki or brandy and was equally
unsuccessful.

Several kelluks or rafts from Mosul for
Baghdad stopped here for their crews to buy
food. They are the favourite mode of travelling
down the river and when, as is often the case,

KUFA OR ROUND BOAT.

they have a sort of cabin or shanty built upon
them, seem to be a very luxurious sort of
conveyance.

We saw here for the first time kufas or round
boats, which have existed in the same form from
prehistoric times, and perhaps gave the idea to

Admiral Popoff of the wondrous ironclads
which are called after his name. These boats
are regular round baskets, made of twigs and·
plastered within and without with bitumen.
Occasionally, we were told, there is a covering
of skins put over the basket-work before the
bitumen is applied ; but we did not see any in
which it was used. The kufas vary very much
in size, some being big enough to carry three
or four horses or bullocks whilst others will
barely contain a couple of men.

Besides the kufas 'there were also a few
boats like those at Bir-ed-jik ; and people also
crossed the rivers on blown-up skins precisely
as may be seen on the bas-reliefs at the British
Museum.

A date-palm growing by the waterside showed
we were approaching warmer climes, and the
next day we saw a whole grove near Dur.
Dur or Dura is famous as being the spot
where Sapor dictated the terms of peace to
the pusillanimous Jovian. Neither general nor
statesman, and harassed by the Arabs who had

revolted from his standard, he was glad to purchase his safety at any price. If Julian had lived it is not much to expect that the course of history would have been altered; certainly he would have preferred sacrificing his life to losing his honour.

As we marched along we could see, flashing in the distance, the gilded dome of a mosque at Samara, which was also a fortified town in the time of Jovian; but we were not destined to reach it the same day. We had now come down on to the great alluvial plain which stretches away to the Persian Gulf, and not a hill was in sight save a mound near Dura and some distant hills to the north-east.

We halted for the night at the camp of some Edlim Arabs, who were moving about in search of pasture; and next morning went on to Samara, or rather to an island in the Tigris opposite Samara, where we pitched our tents. On the way we passed some ruins, called by the Arabs Aschik, which were in a very good state of preservation, though now only a shelter for the jackal and raven.

The building was situated on a mound, with a big ditch and earthworks round it, and itself formed a large quadrangle, the sides facing to the cardinal points, and with large gateways in the centre of the east and west fronts.

The *enceinte* consisted of small square bastions connected by short curtains; on each bastion was a round tower, and these towers were connected by walls with recessed arches in them, separated by flat and half round pilasters. The whole was built of sun-dried bricks with a casing of burnt bricks. Close by was another smaller ruin somewhat of the same description.

For miles along the left bank of the Tigris extended the ruins of ancient towns, all being said by our Arabs to be those of Eski Baghdad, or the ancient Baghdad. A large and lofty tower, surrounded by a spiral road, is said to have been the look-out post of the caliph

Haroun al Raschid, whilst a very large building close to is said to have been his palace.

On the right bank of the river, opposite Samara, there was a certain amount of cultivation being carried on in the rudest manner

PRIMITIVE PLOUGH.

possible by some almost naked Edlim Arabs, who seemed quite a different race from their fellow tribesmen with whom we had passed the previous evening. Their agricultural implements were of the most primitive type. A

plough, consisting of a pointed log of wood,
was held upright by a sort of handle by one
man whilst two others dragged it along,
making a furrow perhaps three inches deep.
Two men were labouring with a wooden rake,
one holding the handle and the other pulling
at a string tied to the crossbar; and a spade
with a blade the size of the palm of one's hand
seemed to be almost too heavy for the man
who used it.   Several bullocks were employed
in raising water, which as the river was low
had to be brought to the foot of the bank in
artificial channels.   Wherever the water was
conducted there was most lush and luxuriant
vegetation; and, as in olden times, three or
four cuttings of fodder are obtained from the
wheat crop before it is allowed to form its ear.
Herodotus says that two and sometimes three
hundredfold rewarded the cultivators in ancient
days, and there can be no doubt that the same
results might be obtained even now.

When our camp was formed we went over
to Samara, crossing the river in a kufa, which,

notwithstanding its peculiar shape, was propelled
at a good pace by a couple of men with paddles.

A new wall of very mean appearance surrounds the town, in the middle of which stands
the mosque, whose gilded dome had been
dazzling us for so long. It stands over the tomb
of one of the twelve Imams, who are regarded
as sacred persons by the Shiah Mohammedans,
and of whom the twelfth is to appear at the end
of the world. The dome was gilded by orders
of the Shah when he made a pilgrimage here
some years ago. A lesser dome and two
minarets are covered with glazed Persian tiles
which form arabesques and flowers. The gilt
dome was surmounted by a blazing sun, with
eyes, nose, and mouth all complete; whilst on
the summit of the smaller one was a moon.
An inner wall surrounds the mosque and its
courtyards, into which we were not allowed to
penetrate, though we could get a glimpse through
the gateways. All seemed to have been once
carefully tiled, and pretty fountains were playing :
but great patches of tiles had peeled off, and,

unless something was done to arrest the action of the weather, it seems as if soon all would be in ruins.

The kaimacan we found to be a Circassian; but though better than his countryman at Tekrit, he was not calculated to improve our opinion of his race. When we asked for a guide to Baghdad, he at first seemed disinclined to provide us with one, and then wanted to saddle us with half a dozen Circassians. At last we got what we wanted, and went back to our tents after a walk round about to see the ruins of Haroun al Raschid's palace and what glimpses we were permitted to get of the mosque.

Inside the walls of the town more than three-fifths of the space is vacant and serves as a camping place for the Persian pilgrims, of whom over thirty thousand are said to visit the place every year.

Close to Samara is the famous Naharwan canal, which, leaving the Tigris below the Hamrin hills, falls into it again ten miles

below Samara at a place called Majaliweh,
opposite to Istabilat.   Opis is supposed to have
been near Samara, and, I think, is most probably
represented by the ruins at Majaliweh.   Cyrus
and Alexander, as well as Sapor and Jovian,
have contributed to the history of this most
important position ; and it was here that Ali,
founder of the sect of the Shiahs,—who, if history
be true, have the most claim to be considered
orthodox Mohammedans—for a long time main-
tained his position as caliph.   On the banks
of the Naharwan he fought the famous battle in
which the sect of the Karegites or separatists,
under Abdallah ibn Waheb their leader, four
thousand in number, were all cut to pieces
except nine (in some accounts seven), whilst Ali
only lost nine (or seven) in all. These survivors
however, were nine too many for Ali's safety ;
for three of them, afterwards meeting at
Meccah, agreed that it would be for the best
interests of Mohammedanism to kill the rival
caliphs and Amrou ibn Aási, the governor
of Egypt. Abdarrahmân ibn Melgem, who

undertook the murder of Ali, found two
other Karegites, Derwan and Shabib, who were
willing to join him, and the three set upon
Ali in the mosque at Kufa, on the seventeenth
day of the month Ramadan A.H. 40, and
wounded him so that he died. Shabib alone
of these three assassins escaped; the other
two were captured and put to death. Moawiyah
was wounded by Barak, who was at first
punished by having his hands and feet cut
off, but was afterwards killed by one of the
friends of Moawiyah. Amrou escaped through
being too ill to go to the mosque at Cairo
on the day agreed upon by the murderers; and
Charijah, who was preaching in his stead, fell
a victim in his place to the poisoned blade of
Amrou ibn Beker.

At Istabilat there are the remains of a large
town, of which the lines of the streets can be
distinctly traced, and the ruins of the fortifications, which consisted of numerous small bastions connected by short curtains, are plainly to
be seen. This fortified town and some smaller

fortifications near, which seem to have been the outworks, were evidently built to defend a large artificial port, which had been constructed at the entrance of a very large canal which here leaves the western side of the river. Istabilat and Majaliweh combined, completely barred the passage of either the Tigris or the canals by a hostile fleet; and hence the size and importance of the ruins.

At Samara our Arab escort had completed their duty, so we gave them a great entertainment, the shaykh and his son joining us at our own table; and in the morning, after most affectionate farewells we parted, they for their own homes, and we for the south and Baghdad.

We rode past the ruins of Istabilat, and then through a perfectly level country intersected by many canals on different levels. Some had small ditches, used to conduct a scanty supply of water to villages and cultivated ground, cleared out in their centres.

We crossed the principal low-level canal on a bridge lately constructed by Ferhan

Pasha to give access to a settlement he has
formed of Jemmar Arabs, from the Eastern
bank of the Tigris, who cultivate the ground
for him.   Near this we camped, and found
that the water had to be drawn from a well
some forty feet deep, supplied most probably
by filtration from the river.   These Jemmar
were inhospitable and low caste Arabs, like
most who have given up the free life of the
desert and become tillers of the soil.

Next day we were not sorry to leave this
place, and after crossing a large canal on a
bridge called Jisr Hartha, we came upon a
tract where there were several villages, all
surrounded by groves of date-palms and fig-
trees, and with numerous small canals running
in different directions, and numerous little
domed tombs showing the resting-place of
prophets or saints.   After a short march we
camped at one of the date-surrounded towns
called Sumeischah, the next halting-place being
Khan Suediyah, and six hours distant.

This little town Sumeischah had only a

population of a hundred and seventy-five adult
males, yet it sends away annually twenty thousand okes (each 2·85 lbs.) of dates besides figs
and corn.   The tax collector and mudir were
civil, and came to call on us and offered to do
anything that they could to assist us.

Having had a short day, we took advantage
of the afternoon to try and get some sort of
respectability into the appearance of our saddles
and bridles, and scrubbed and polished away
as if we were possessed.   Our servants could not
make out what was the use of polishing bits
and stirrups, and when set to work to do it
were very languid in their endeavours.

From Sumeischah to Khan Suediyah the
country was uncultivated and bare ; but in a few
places where rainwater had lodged, grass was
growing green and fresh.   Near one of these
spots was a santon's tomb, under the shade of
which we sat down to wait for the mules, which as
usual were lagging behind ; and in front of us,
whilst sitting smoking, we suddenly saw four
gazelle come from behind a mound which marked

the line of an ancient canal. We had neither
dogs nor rifles with us ; so, leaving Schaefer and
Gabriel to watch proceedings, I stole quietly out
of sight and hearing with my horse, and then
mounting I clapped in my spurs and rode for
the caravan to get my Henry rifle. I snatched
it from the man carrying it, and was away
again before the people could make out
what I wanted ; and luckily, as it turned out,
their cowardice instantly made them imagine
robbers, so they halted and after a bit turned
back.

When I got back to where I had left
Schaefer and Gabriel, I found the gazelle had
got behind another mound, and by working
up carefully I was able to bag the buck.

When I came back to the horses there was
no caravan in sight, so I climbed up to the top
of the tomb and saw them all in full retreat,
the report of the rifle having been too much
for their weak nerves. If they had come
on they would most likely have startled the
game, so it was as well they did not. Gabriel

was despatched to bring them up, and caught
them up after a regular chase. He said when he
came back that the mules had never travelled
so fast in their lives before. Having got one
gazelle, I thought we might perhaps find more
and kept on the look out. Several times the
mirage deceived me, and I only found out after
half an hour's or more patient creeping and crawl-
ing that I had been stalking a camel, a sheep, or
a goat. Once it was even more ludicrous. I saw
an animal, which I made sure was a gazelle,
standing near what I thought was a large white
stone. I stealthily stole along behind a bank
and then went up on my hands and knees,
making certain of a good shot, when I saw
the stone get up and mount the gazelle. It was
a pilgrim praying beside his donkey, who had
just finished as I got within distance. After
this I thought it best to give up shooting for
the day.

When we arrived at Khan Suediyah we found
no one there except an Arab family, and were
therefore able to establish ourselves and our

animals comfortably.   About three in the afternoon however large caravans of Persian pilgrims ,
bound for Samara began to arrive, and by sunset the whole place was crowded.   Many
travelled with a great deal of comfort, having
wives and servants with them ; whilst others
were poor and could only afford to hire a share
in a mule.   Besides the living pilgrims, there
were a number of corpses being brought by
their friends to inter in the neighbourhood of
the holy place.   A mule usually carried two live
pilgrims or one live man and two dead bodies.
All night long there was noisy praying, varied
by squabbles and fights round the fires that
they had made for cooking, so that we were
not sorry when daylight appeared and we
were able to start for Baghdad.

Schaefer and I went on with one zaptieh,
leaving the mules to follow after.   We soon
came upon the river Tigris, and passed much
cultivation, all irrigated by water raised by
bullocks.   Near Kansimain we met many more
pilgrims, and then soon came into gardens

which extended the whole way to Baghdad.
Here we were astonished by the sight of a
tramway which had been constructed by Midhat
Pasha, when Wali of Baghdad, to connect Kansimain with the town.   Crossing the bridge of
boats, our eyes were gladdened by the sight of
the Union Jack waving over the Residency,
and the blue ensign flying on board the Bombay
Marine steamer *Comet*.   Just before we got
into the Residency we met Mr. Cuthbert, one
of the officers of the *Comet*, whom I had known
during the Abyssinian campaign.

At the Residency we were most kindly welcomed by Colonel and Mrs. Nixon, and found
under their hospitable roof Mr. and Lady Anne
Blunt, who had arrived from Damascus after a
most plucky and adventurous journey through
Northern Nejd.   The Blunts were to start the
same night for a visit to a chief of the Bak-
tiari Kurds in the mountains beyond Shuster;
and we made an agreement to meet them if
possible at Bunder Abbas, where, according to
their then intentions, Lady Anne was to take

steamer for India whilst her husband and ourselves would go on by land.

They made the journey by land to Bushire, but the season was then too far advanced for travelling by land along the shores of the Persian Gulf; whilst, although I did not then know it, my land journey was to finish at Baghdad.

We, as soon as possible, began to try to buy camels for the remainder of our intended journey, and to engage fresh servants as our Syrian followers would go no further than Baghdad.

Whilst busied about these preparations news came of the fatal day at Isandula. Of course details were scanty, but it seemed to me as if I might be of use; and finding that by starting that night by the *Blosse Lynch* I could catch the steamer at Basrah, which corresponded at Aden with the mail for Zanzibar and Natal; my preparations were made almost as quickly as my resolution was taken; and the next morning I and my horses were steaming down the Tigris. At Basrah I found the B. I. steamer *Patna*, commanded by an old Abyssinian friend, James Avern—I am sure that his name and that of his ship, *Euphrates*, No. 1. of the transport fleet, are familiar to almost all who were in Ansley Bay in 1868—was that by which I should have to take passage. We started the morning after the arrival of the *Blosse Lynch*, and reached Karachi after a short stay at Bushire, "the father of ports," without any incident.

Here we were to stay for a few days, and the members of the Scind Club, with great kindness and hospitality, made me an honorary member during my sojourn among them, and added to their kindness by giving me a dinner before I left. Scarcely had I taken up my quarters at the club when I received a telegram,—laconic, but fatal to my hopes of joining in the Zulu campaign,—"Admiralty forbids." Obedience being one's first duty, I sold my horses and took my ticket to

London instead of Natal. A pleasant though
uneventful voyage, rendered pleasanter by
agreeable companions, landed me in England
on the 29th of May. On reporting my arrival
to "their lordships," and my reasons for returning, I found that the telegram had been
sent under a misapprehension of their intentions
and that leave had been granted me to go to
the Cape. It was then, however, too late to
hope for much chance of seeing service; so I
reluctantly gave up, the idea of going out and,
instead, busied myself with writing this account
of a very enjoyable journey along what I trust·
·may prove "Our Future Highway" to India
·and the East.

CHAPTER XIV.

THE question of railway communication with
India is a very large and important one to this
country; and, as many rival routes are compet-
ing for the prime position amongst our future
highways between Occident and Orient, it is
very necessary that we should judge fairly,
dispassionately, and calmly of the various
advantages and disadvantages which belong to
each.

It is generally considered as an axiom that it is to local, not through traffic, the promoters of a railway must look for its principal revenue. It is also an almost universally admitted fact that, all other things being equal, the route which gives the maximum of railway and the minimum of sea-passage is best for the transport of mails, passengers, and small articles of merchandise of high intrinsic value.

The physical configuration of the country through which a railway would pass—its water-supply, local supply of labour and its price, the facility of feeding the labourer, the present means of transport available for the conveyance of plant and material are all important questions to consider before deciding on the construction of a line.

It is also of great importance that a railway should, if possible, have both its termini under the same government; or at least that, as far as can be arranged, as few frontiers as possible should be crossed on its track, on account of passport, custom-house, and quarantine

.regulations, which at any time may be exercised vexatiously by a neutral power without actually causing a *casus belli*.

Our present route, *viâ* Brindisi, to the Mediterranean, possesses many advantages over one to Constantinople, as it lies outside the theatre of the Eastern question and through the territory of powers whose interest in the Mediterranean render them averse to the formation of a new naval power in its waters, and who identified their interests with our own in the Crimea. To reach Constantinople we should have to pass through France, Belgium, the German Empire, Austria (whose future is the most difficult question in the Eastern question), Servia and Bulgaria (who at any moment might be stirred up against us by Russian agents), and thence through Turkish territory to Constantinople.

In times of peace, Constantinople might, no doubt, be reached, when connected with the European system of railways, well nigh as easily as Brindisi. Then by a railway from

Scutari to the Persian Gulf, the only frontier
to be crossed would be the Turko-Persian,
where no difficulties need be apprehended, as
we should, unless our power declines very
much, always be strong enough to face the
question of an alliance between Russia and
Persia.

Perhaps it would be best to enumerate the
lines proposed by various authorities and interests as being, according to them, the most
advantageous for connecting the West and
the East :—

1st. The Russian scheme, *viâ* Orenburg, to
have one terminus in India and the other on
the Baltic; also advocated by Monsieur de
Lesseps.

2nd. *Viâ* Constantinople, Diarbekr, and
Mosul to Baghdad and the Persian Gulf.

3rd. From Iskanderûn to Aleppo, and by
the Euphrates Valley to Kweyt (Grane).

4th. From Tripoli, *viâ* Palmyra, to Baghdad
or Kweyt.

5th. From Tyre to Kweyt or Basrah.

6th. From Sidon to Damascus, and thence to Baghdad or Kweyt.

7th. A line from El Arish to Kweyt or Basrah.

8th. A line using Seleucia as the seaport.

9th. A line which, after Aleppo, should pass by Mosul to Teheran, Herat, Kabul, and the Khyber Pass to Attock.

10th. From Tripoli to Homs, Hamah, Mara, Idlib, Aleppo, Urfa, under Mardin, Nisibin, Mosul, and then by the valley of the Tigris to Baghdad, thence to Bushire, and in some future time by Laristan and Beluchistan to Karachi.

The first may be briefly dismissed as being of no political use to India ; commercially it would, no doubt, open a market for our tea ; and deal a great blow to the Chinese overland trade with Russia. A very large portion would pass through desert tracks and regions only inhabited by nomad tribes, who would con-tribute nothing to the local traffic, which is as necessary to a railway as bread is to man. If the Russians construct it as far as Merv we need not be unduly afraid of its military consequences; as, though it might assist them in keeping order in their newly-acquired territories, no railway of such enormous length would be equal to the strain of keeping up the supplies necessary for an army sufficiently strong to make even a hostile demonstration against our Indian frontier. Our greatest danger, if any exists, is the co-operation of Russia and Persia, using the Caspian as a base on the flank of our communication with India *via* the Persian Gulf.

With regard to the second, we have already seen that the European route to Constantinople has many disadvantages when compared with the mail route to Brindisi. For the products of Turkey in Asia, Constantinople is also disadvantageously situated in comparison with any of the Ports of Syria or the Mediterranean coast of Asia Minor, both as necessitating a longer sea voyage and also a more dangerous navigation.

The line has been taken in hand and abandoned several times, the section between Scutari and Ismidt being all that is completed—where, no doubt, it is of use, but which is merely a link in the connection between Constantinople and a favourite watering-place. Near Angora, ruined earthworks remain, monuments of those who undertook a task without counting the cost. Surveys have been made for some portions of the line, but that they are still in existence is a matter of much doubt. Indeed, what has been done is of a piece with the other public works in Turkey in Asia. Commenced by one to be neglected by another, and usually to fall into ruinous disrepair ere completed. Even the few honest officials who have, according to their lights struggled to do something for the country, have always commenced some new undertaking which might recommend itself to their fancy rather than complete works begun by their predecessors,—and so the railway has been commenced and abandoned half a dozen times already.

The mountainous nature of the country in Asia Minor proper would render the construction of any railway costly both in time and money, and would afterwards require more money for its working and maintenance in proper repair than one constructed in regions where the engineering difficulties were less.

Strategically this line would not be of any great utility, for any future advance of the Russians on Constantinople will be by a route in easy communication with the Black Sea, as, even if a feint were made against Constantinople from the North, they would not break their heads against the lines of Tchatchaldja when the capital might be forced to capitulate by an enemy possessing Armenia and Eastern Anatolia, without a shot having been fired against its fortifications. The Anti-Taurus would at first protect the line, but if reached by them at Angora, the war would be practically over. Of course, if the Russians are

unable to hold the command of the Black
Sea, they might be much hampered by columns
landed on the coast; but the people are not
unfriendly to them, owing to the way in which
their troops were kept in hand and all supplies
promptly paid for during the last war, and
their agents are everywhere busy in under-
mining the Turkish authority and fanning
sedition and discontent which, were the people
not amongst the most patient in the world,
would soon burst into flame.

The cost of the line from Scutari to Diarbekr
would prove greater than that of any other
route except the first and eighth, and therefore
on that account alone would have to be left
until the trade of the country is more developed
and the government more able to assist in such
an undertaking, as there can be no greater mistake in political economy than to overweight
a struggling population with costly public
works for the benefit of their successors.

The third route has, on first sight, much
to recommend it. Iskanderûn, being the

nearest port to Aleppo, has for centuries possessed most of the trade of that great emporium, is well known to Europeans, and the line to Kweyt is comparatively short. But, on considering the matter more attentively, we are forced to abandon it, owing to the unhealthiness of the town, the engineering difficulties to be surmounted in crossing the Beilan Pass and the swamp at its back; besides which the whole valley of the Euphrates below Bir-ed-jik is well-nigh uncultivated, and almost the only population are nomad Arabs who would add nothing to the local traffic, thus rendering the whole section from Aleppo to Kweyt dependent on the through traffic, which, as before stated would not prove sufficient to maintain the line. Using Kweyt would also be taking the terminus of the line to the wrong side of the Persian Gulf, because some day, no doubt, India will complete the whole line, and then the section from Deir *viâ* Babylon, to Kweyt would be useless.

In the fourth scheme, we have at Tripoli

the advantages of a good roadstead, where a grand harbour might be easily constructed, the easiest pass through the mountains by which the level country in the interior may be reached, and a comparatively short line to construct.   Fifteen miles east of Homs the country is all uncultivated, and there is no local traffic to be anticipated for many years.   Baghdad, though it may be, nay, is sure to be, a station and an important one on the line, will never do for a terminus, as the navigation of the Tigris thence to Basrah is tedious and difficult and can never be depended on with that degree of certainty which is required for a line conveying important mails.   Though at present it is not desirable to construct this portion of the line, there can be little doubt that many now living will see it working, and not only working but paying.   Against Kweyt the same objections hold good as in the third scheme.

The fifth scheme has the support in part of no less an authority than Captain Burton, but

the absence of local traffic again proves an
insuperable obstacle.   Basrah would be a good
temporary terminus, were it not for the difficulty and cost of carrying the line over the
swampy ground near the river.   Kweyt has
already been disposed of.   This line, in common with all going direct across the Mesopotamian desert, would entail the digging of wells
to supply the workmen employed on the line
with water.   The valley of the Jordan would
also have to be passed, which would be a great
engineering obstacle.

The sixth, from Sidon (Saida) to Damascus,
possesses no advantages as to distance or
traffic over the lines which would have Tripoli
as their terminus, and the country between
Sidon and Damascus is so mountainous and
rocky as to render the construction of a railway
very costly and difficult.   Sidon has a small
harbour, but to render it fit for such a traffic
as there would be at the terminus of the Indo-
Mediterranean line would entail an enormous
cost.

The seventh, from El Arish to Kweyt, would be the shortest line between the Mediterranean and Persian Gulf, but the desert nature of the country prevents its being suitable for the construction of a railway.

The eighth only differs from the first in using Seleucia as a port; the old harbour, however, has been silted up, and would besides; even if dredged out, be very small for modern ships to make use of, and the River Orontes would have to be bridged no less than seventeen times in twenty-one miles.

The ninth, as far as Mosul, is the same as the tenth, which we will examine more closely immediately. Beyond Mosul, as the civilisation and trade of the countries to be passed through develops, so will the necessity of a railway become more urgent. Afghanistan,[1] it is hoped,

---

[1] This was written before the dastardly murder of our envoy had shocked the whole civilised world, and our punitive campaign had commenced. The line now proposed to Kandahar will no doubt form one of the links in the chain of communication which the events of the last few months prove to be imperatively necessary.

since the settlement of the differences with the
Government óf India and the appointment of
British Residents, will rapidly improve; but
Persia is, I suppose, the worst-governed country
in the world—worse even than Turkey or a
small South American republic : her future will
depend largely upon the action of both England and Russia, and it is to be hoped that no
undue jealousy of the other's influence on the
part of either may prevent whatever schemes
may be mooted for her improvement.

The tenth and last scheme is the one which
seems to promise most for the future. The
local traffic already existing is very considerable
and would almost immediately increase enor-
mously, and there are many other reasons why
it should be the line to be first constructed.

Commencing with Tripoli as the Mediterranean terminus, we find many and great advantages, one of the most prominent of which
is its healthiness and another the abundant
supply of good water.

Tripoli at present consists of one of the three

Greek towns which gave it its name, and the seaside suburb of El Mina, close to the anchorage; these two are connected by a good road about two miles in length, along which a diligence travels three or four times a day. His Excellency, Midhat Pasha, has already placed a line of trams on this road.

There are now two good roadsteads, one perfectly sheltered from all winds except those from the north and east, and even in these quite safe for ships to lie at anchor in, though in heavy gales communication with the shore would be difficult; the other would only be used by ships wishing to communicate with the shore during the prevalence of the above winds, as it is open to all those from the westward.

The natural configuration of the land would immensely facilitate the formation of a port in the first-named of the two roadsteads amply sufficient for the trade which would spring up. Limestone and other materials for building the necessary jetties and breakwater are all close at hand, and labour is cheap and abundant.

The present trade of the port is mostly local, consisting principally of fruit from the gardens round the town and grain from the districts near Homs and Hamah ; but nevertheless the exports even now amount to upwards of thirteen million francs per annum.   This trade has great capabilities and might be almost indefinitely extended, as large tracts of well-watered and fertile land are lying fallow, owing to the want of transport.

The line which I should propose for the railway would follow the level country between the mountains and the sea, till, after passing the Nahr el Barid and Nahr el Kebir, and then pass through them by the Wadys Eyne Soodi and Kara Chibôk to the Bukéa, a small and wondrously fertile plain nearly encircled by the Nahr el Kebir, and after about three miles of rather difficult work, for the passing of which there might be some engineering required, by natural gradients to the plains around Homs. Here the Nahr el Asy (Orontes) would have to be crossed, but a bridge of sixty feet in

length, with approaches on either side of about
a hundred yards, would be amply sufficient.

Homs (the ancient Emessa), was once one
of those wonderfully rich cities which were
dotted about these plains, but which, owing
to the substitution of Saracen for Christian
power, and later on by the blight which seems
to rest on all under the Turkish rule, has
dwindled down to a town of between twenty
and twenty-five thousand inhabitants.

The waters of the Orontes are used in some
measure for the irrigation of the gardens near
the town, which extend over a space of four
to four and a half miles in width. Grain even
now is sent down to the coast in great quantities, but the rates of carriage are so high,
and so much is lost in the wet season (fully
ten per cent.) owing to the camels falling in
the mud and breaking their limbs, that an
immediate increase could be looked for in
this trade. Silk and cotton are produced
and manufactured to a considerable extent,
but the greater portion is used in the country

and not exported. If cheap means of transport were available much of this would be exported, and fabrics more fitted to the use of the peasantry introduced.

The hire of a camel, whose load is a quarter of a ton, is from sixty to seventy piastres to Tripoli, a distance of fifty miles in a straight line, and sixty by the present road, and seventy by the best line for a railway. Now the mileage rates are tenpence a ton at the very least, and any railway could afford to convey goods for a third of that amount. Other branches of cultivation might be easily developed if good government could be guaranteed and the capital lying idle in the country employed. The capital hidden away all over Turkey in Asia must be very large, as the imports do not average more than two-thirds of the exports in value. Sugar, coffee, and many of the minor luxuries of life (necessities according to European ideas), are almost unknown to the peasantry and poorer population of towns on account of their cost. They know them sufficiently well to long for them, but are debarred from using them by the high prices, and if they could get a better and readier market for their own produce, would at once become large consumers, not only of these small luxuries, but also of European products and manufactures, such as soft goods, hardware, and crockery.

From Homs to Hamah the line would not necessitate any engineering works beyond the levelling of the ground to place the rails and sleepers, and then ballasting them, except at Rusta where the Orontes flows through a deep valley, in some places widening out to three or four miles, in others becoming a mere gorge or ravine. The road now passes by Rusta, where there was once a Roman station which was evidently considered of much importance. The descent on the right side of the river is gradual till within about three hundred and fifty yards of the river, where there is a sudden break down to the small level space fringing the stream. Here would be the first piece of

work requiring any engineering talent after
rising from the plain of the Bukéa. The
present bridge across the river, including part
which acts as a dam with a mill erected on
it, is four hundred feet in all, while the natural
width of the stream is two hundred.

On the left side the land rises rather
abruptly, and the cheapest way to overcome
the difficulty would seem to be a viaduct across
the bottom of the valley, four to five hundred
yards in length, and fifty feet high at the
highest, which would come more than half
way up the left side. Thence; either a curve
round the face of the slope, such as the road
makes at present, or a cutting of about half
a mile to join the viaduct by a gentle slope
to the plain beyond. This cutting would be
forty or fifty feet deep at the commencement
running to nothing at the end, and the earth
might be utilised for an embankment for part
of the distance, instead of making the viaduct
reach right across the bottom of the valley.

After this cutting nothing more would be

required to Hamah, the natural gradients being
so easy that it would not be worth while to
improve them. At Hamah the Orontes is
met again, but may be crossed on the level;
the bridge over it is now two hundred feet
long, but much of this is used to dam up
the river to work a flour-mill and big water-
wheels which raise the water for irrigating
the gardens of the town.

Beyond Hamah the country is level, and
the only thing to be done would be the bridging of three ravines between it and Tyiby,
of which the largest would require an arch
with a span of twenty feet with approaches
of forty yards on either side. Between Tyiby.
and our next station at Khan Shaykh Khaun
the country is still level, but there is one
widish ravine which would require a bridge
of some little length to allow torrent-water to
pass, and an embankment on each side; but
the whole width to be covered is not over
five or six hundred yards. Thence to Khan
Shaykh Khaun it is all quite level.

From Khan Shaykh Khaun to Mara the
country rises and falls again, but by a very
small detour the necessity of making any earthworks would be avoided, and again the same is
the case as far as Idlib or Sarmeen.

From Idlib to Zurby, though the maps show
a range of hills, there is a perfectly level road
by making a very small detour, and thence
to the river Alep there is only one gentle
rise. At Khan Tomaun the ordinary road
to Aleppo branches off from the line we have
been following, and goes over some steep
rocky hills, but by following the course of the
stream a level and easy way is found close
to Aleppo.

The whole distance between Tripoli and
Aleppo by this route is as follows :

	Line.	Direct.
Tripoli to Homs	70 miles.	50 miles.
Homs to Hamah	30 ,,	29 ,,
Hamah to Mara	39 ,,	34 ,,
Mara to Idlib	26 ,,	24 ,,
Idlib to Aleppo	32 ,,	28 ,
Total	197	165

From Alexandretta to Aleppo is fifty-seven
miles direct; by the line a railway would have
to take ninety-seven miles, in which the Beilan
Pass would have to be crossed at a vast expen-
diture of time, labour and money. In fact I
do believe that the cost of crossing the Beilan
alone would be more than that of the whole
line from Tripoli to Aleppo, and the works
would occupy a period of nine or ten years.

The traffic as given me at various points,
viz., at Homs, Hamah and Mara, on the spot,
and at Sarmeen for Idlib, now amounts to
nearly two thousand camels or four hundred
tons per diem, which would none of it, except
perhaps that from Idlib, ever be taken to the
line between Aleppo and Iskanderûn, whilst
the whole of it would be immediately available
for the proposed line, without taking into
consideration the carrying trade of Aleppo,
which employs eighty thousand camels.

The whole of this trade might be calculated
as having an average distance at the present
time of eighty miles to travel to find a port of

shipment, and costing 240,000*l.* per annum for its transit.

N.B.—Much now goes to Latakia and Iskanderûn.

If a line were constructed for 10,000*l.*, a mile, and the same mileage charged, this would give an interest of over twelve per cent. for purely local traffic; but, though a line would be obliged to carry cheaper, it surely would not be too much to calculate on a line paying five per cent. after working expenses were defrayed.

From Aleppo onwards the line at first would follow a nearly level route to Mombedj, a distance, as the line would have to run, of forty miles. From Mombedj to near the embouchure of the Nahr Sadschur, which would be the best point for crossing the Euphrates, is only twelve miles more; and thence to Haran, the first fifteen miles alone would be difficult, and even there, by a little judgment, all serious earthworks would be avoided. The detours necessary would probably

increase the distance to twenty miles. Thirty-
five to thirty-seven more miles would bring us
to Haran, situated on the same level plain as
Urfa, a city of great commercial importance.
If it is thought best for the line to actually go
to Urfa, or only pass close by, it would make a
difference of fifteen miles, i.e. the line would
either go twenty miles to Urfa and then twelve
and a half miles to Khan Medscheri, or direct
seventeen and a half miles to Khan Medscheri.
Perhaps a branch to Urfa would be best. After
Khan Medscheri the first ten miles is very
slightly hilly; but then to Tel Armen (below
Mardin), Nisibin, Tchil Agha, Roumeilat, and
to within seven miles of Mosul—a distance in all
of two hundred and twenty miles—the country
is quite level, except for about seven or eight
miles of the distance between Asmaur and
Tschil Agha, where either a small detour might
be advisable or some earthworks would be
required.

Three hundred and forty miles would thus be
about the distance required between Aleppo

and Mosul ; and, allowing for the bridge over
the Euphrates, the whole ought easily to
be constructed on the same scale as our
European railways—at 5,000*l.* a mile, because
it is scarcely to be conceived that there is
another tract of country in the world of equal
extent offering such unparalleled facilities for
the construction of a railway.

From Mosul to Baghdad the line should
follow nearly the right bank of the Tigris as
far as Samara, and then straight to Baghdad.
The whole distance is one hundred and eighty
miles and, allowing for curves, might possibly
amount to two hundred.

Leaving Mosul, we first should go along the
level of the plain the town is built on for five
miles, and then for two miles, commencing at
El Kasr, cuttings and earthworks would be
necessary. A dead level would then be
traversed till after passing Hammam Ali, and
when opposite Nimrud, a distance of nine miles
more, a slope a mile and a half in length would
have to be ascended and another level reached.

The distance between the two levels is about
fifty feet, which would give a gradient of nearly
one in one hundred and fifty.

The upper level being reached, it would be
kept on for about eighteen miles; a small
amount of levelling and embankment might be
required here and there, and occasional culverts
to allow the flood-water from the Sinjar and
other hills to the westward [1] to find its way to
the river.   After this plain had been passed a
couple of miles of descent would have to be
worked across, which would bring the line to the
ower level again, where a wady which conveys
a good deal of water to the Tigris would have to
be crossed ; it varies in width and, although it is
only ten feet deep and from six to twenty feet
wide, would have to have its banks levelled
for some distance to the westward to prevent
its altering its course and damaging the road.

---

[1] Halfway across was an old canal which rejoins the river
at Sherghat ; this was thirty feet wide, with banks fifteen feet
high raised above the plain.   The river must once have
run in a higher bed, or large hydraulic works been used to
fill this canal.

Here is a permanent camp of Jebour Arabs, who might always be depended on to furnish a cheap supply of labour.

Leaving this camp, the next mile and a half was a dead level, with one small water channel three feet deep by six wide ; and then, after a mile of small rises and bitumen beds and sulphur springs, another level plain is reached, which, without engineering work of any sort being required, takes us to Jernaf, where more Jebours are settled, a distance of ten miles. Five miles from Jernaf the upper level juts, in a sort of promontory, out on the lower till close to the river, and the track now goes up a wady and then across broken ground till the lower level is reached on the other side. A cutting fifty feet deep for half a mile would run through this projection. Fifty feet would be the greatest depth required, but the tongue of land is so *accidenté* that the quantity of earth to be removed would not be more than if the whole distance was calculated for a depth of twenty or thirty feet.

After this promontory, two miles of perfectly
level ground takes us to _Sherghat, the head-
quarters of Ferhan Pasha, who is recognised
as head shaykh of the Jebel Shammar by the
Turkish Government. From Sherghat, a level
for one and a half miles, crossing a nullah, and
then a gradual ascent of sixty feet in three miles
more, brought us to an open plain, with low hills
between it and the river, and drained to the
westward by a shallow valley. After six miles
on this plain, the valley which had received the
drainage comes to an end, and a series of wadys
break away to the river just north of the
Hamrin hills. Four miles across these wadys
and the small intervening hills (which are
called Bel-a-dij by the Arabs) would require
some cutting and bridging. The next twenty-
four miles was dead level, only intersected by
four small nullahs, none of which would require
a bridge of over twenty feet in length. At the
end of this plain is a small salt stream about ten
feet wide and two deep, and then after a mile
through low sand hills from ten to fifteen feet

in height, another three miles brings one abreast
of Kala'at Mekrun.   Here hills bounded
the plain, which varies from two miles to a
quarter of a mile in width ; and after ten and a
half miles more the river and hills approach
each other, and then a rise of seventy feet has
to be made in about a mile and a half, intersected by small wadys, one large one of a
hundred and fifty feet in width finishing the
series, and then the upper plain is reached.

Twelve miles along the upper plain brings
the road abreast of Tekrit.   Three miles more,
and another wady has to be crossed, and then
after one mile more and another wady, the
great alluvial plain of the Tigris is reached.
Once on this plain the only obstacles to be
encountered before reaching Baghdad are the
remains of the ancient canals and the modern
irrigation works ; by keeping a short distance
from the river the latter may be avoided altogether, and of the former only two would
require bridging.

Up to this point I have spoken from personal

knowledge, but of the portion of country between Baghdad and Bushire I can only speak
from report.

After bridging the Tigris at Baghdad the
country is all nearly level; near Haweizeh
several small bridges would be required, and
one large one over the Karun. The Persian
Gulf should be approached near Dilam, and
the coast line approximately followed to
Bushire.

Bushire is situated on a peninsula, the
isthmus connecting which with the mainland
is overflowed by the tide to a depth of two
or three feet at high water, for a distance of
nearly three miles, where a viaduct would be
required.

Between Baghdad and Bushire, a distance
of four hundred and sixty-eight miles, about
twenty bridges would be required, and these
would be the only engineering works necessary
besides the viaduct across the isthmus.

Material can be transported by steamer to
Baghdad, and also up the Karun as far as

it may be required, and the expense of its
transport materially diminished.

At present there is only an open roadstead
at Bushire, as the bar has too little water on it
for sea-going steamers to cross ; but a channel
of less than half a mile in length might easily
be dredged, and then thirty feet of water is found·
up to and alongside the landing-place, where
a quay might be made for mail steamers to go,
right alongside the railway station.

In no part of the world would a railway have
such important political and commercial results
as the Indo-Mediterranean, whose future course
I have in these pages endeavoured to trace ;
in scarcely any would a line of such length and
importance meet with so few physical difficulties
to be overcome, and be constructed at so small
a cost, and with so great a prospect of financial
success.

CHAPTER XV.

IN the last chapter we have mainly discussed
the physical difficulties which are against and
the facilities which would aid in constructing
a line between the Mediterranean and the
Persian Gulf. To every one, however, who
studies the subject, the question will arise
how the financial and political obstacles are to

be faced and overcome. No one I suppose will deny, that if such a line were constructed and became a financial success, that it would be of immense benefit, not only to our Indian possessions, but also to the inhabitants of the countries through which it would pass.

Everywhere during our journey we found the people anxious for the construction of roads and railways; and at Tripoli, Urfa, Diarbekr and elsewhere, we found people of wealth and position who were willing not only to aid in their construction by moral support, but who would also invest money in the undertaking. All power of initiative has however been crushed out of the mass of the people; and it will be necessary for the inception of public works that support be found in Western Europe.

I have lately heard from Constantinople that a number of *entrepreneurs* and promoters of companies are there, all trying to get concessions for railways and other public works in different parts of the Asiatic dominions of the Sultan, but that most of these people are needy speculators

who only want the grants they ask for in
order to make money for themselves, and so
that they can line their pockets are perfectly
indifferent as to whether railways are ever
constructed or not.

The Russian influence in the councils of the
Porte is now stronger than it has been for
many years, indeed any cabinet of which
Mahmoud Nedim is a member may be considered to all intents and purposes as being
formed of Russian nominees. Since Mahmoud's
accession to power Midhat Pasha has resigned
his post as Wali of Damascus, and it is to be
feared that the public works he has commenced
are therefore doomed, like so many others, never
to be completed. Midhat Pasha no doubt
has faults, and is often too arbitrary in his
proceedings ; being easily flattered, he is also
easily persuaded that whatever he is induced to
undertake is the right thing to do, and therefore
when embarked on any undertaking it is almost
hopeless to try to persuade him to abandon it,
even though it may be costly and useless. To

his honour it may be said that he is honest, and, as far as he understands it, a true patriot ; he is also a staunch friend, and liberal in his religious ideas.

If he could be induced to continue at Damascus, and was placed under the influence of judicious European advisers, if, for instance, our consul-general were moved from Beirut to the seat of government of the province, and he thoroughly understood what reforms were necessary, and had tact and judgment in placing them before Midhat, a very great deal might be accomplished.

But reforming one province would of course be of little use whilst the empire is rotten at the core, and no reforms can be instituted, or if instituted, expected to succeed, until we have reformed the central administration.

Whilst the seraglio clique, in all its abomination, continues *de facto* to govern Turkey, so long will all our endeavours to improve the general state of the country prove futile.

Unfortunately there has never since the days

of "the great Elchi" been an English ambassador at Constantinople of sufficient strength
of mind and force of character for his word to
be law to the Turks. The vital interest which
the future of the Turkish Empire must prove
to the British nation demands that our influence, whilst matters are in their present
chaotic state, should be paramount.

What the future is to be it is difficult to fore-
tell. Austria standing as sentinel at the gates
might well be trusted to garrison the whole
fortress. If Roumania, Servia, and Bulgaria
are to retain their independence or autonomy,
they should be members of a confederation
strong enough to hold its own, unassisted,
against Russia, or any other power that might
attack them. All three combined cannot hope
to do that, with any probability of being successful, and the greatest hope for their future
would lie in their forming part of a federal
alliance of which Austria should be the nominal
head. If this confederation were formed there
would be no objection to granting the demands

of Greece for a rectification of her frontier. Eastern Roumelia and the territory around Constantinople might remain the dominions of the Sultan, but reforms should be carried out and not spoken about; or the country should be administered either by a European commission in the Sultan's name, or else formed into another state belonging to the confederation of the Balkan peninsula.

It seems strange that the Sultan should be regarded as a "divine right" sovereign even by those who most of all argue for succession to a throne remaining in one family. It is entirely contrary to the primitive teaching of the Mohammedan religion that the Kalifate should be an hereditary dignity; and even if it be conceded that it is allowable to alter the dogmas to the extent of substituting a family for an elective succession, how the illegitimate children of illegitimate fathers can be conceived to be the rightful owners of the throne of Othman passes my comprehension. It is known that ever since the days of Bajazet I., that is, during a period of

five centuries, only two sultans have ever been
legally married. What relationship the present
family may possess to the founder of the
Ottoman dynasty, Ertoghrul the right-hearted,
it is difficult to calculate. The harems have
been recruited from all parts where the Turkish
arms have been successful, and of late years
have almost entirely been composed of Circassian
slaves and venal beauties belonging to the
western nations. I have heard a rumour, which
I give for what it may be worth, that the
Russians supply members to the seraglio who
are content to live in splendid infamy in consideration of the high pay given them by the
ministers of the Czar for information regarding
that invisible government which so often baffles
Western diplomacy.

What possible fitness can the ill-educated
child of a slave mother, nurtured in an atmo-
sphere of vice, flattered and fawned upon by
those around him, whilst carefully kept from
the knowledge of the world of politics—what
possible fitness, I say, can such a one have

acquired for the position of a despotic ruler of men ?

Given all the natural abilities and good qualities conceivable—though if heredity is to count for anything it is doubtful if any survive— no child brought up as the children of the Sultan are brought up can pass through such an existence of entire absence of moral or mental control, and indulgence in vicious physical propensities, without being debased, mentally and actually.

If the Turks, or the people spoken of as Turks, are content to be ruled by a person all the blazons of whose escutcheon are blotted and blurred by the bar sinister of bastardy, perhaps it is no business of ours to interfere with them and to alter the custom of centuries; but at the same time we should not deceive ourselves, and believe, because a degenerate debauchee of the nineteenth century has been girded with the sabre of Othman, he is therefore and thereby endowed with the noble qualities of the founders of the Ottoman dynasty.

When we hear praise of the Sultan—that
he is a good ruler, and that it is only because
circumstances are too strong for him that he
does not carry out reforms, we are inclined
to ask if the age of miracles has again appeared
on earth, for nothing short of a miracle could
account for the moral rehabilitation of the
inmate of a harem and a prison, implied in
such phrases.

The evil is there and we must face it boldly ;
we have such a habit in England of making
ourselves believe what we wish to believe,
that we are constantly deceived ; and we also,
as a foreign diplomatist once said to me, enjoy
being deceived.

So now we wish the Sultan of Turkey to
be a talented and able man, virtuous, just, and
honest ; and we hug to our hearts the belief
that he is what we desire ; the awakening will
come, and no' one will be to blame but we
ourselves.

The contrast between the scene of a
sovereign receiving the insignia of one of

Europe's proudest and most exclusive orders amidst the thunder of the cannon of the mightiest fleet that the world had ever seen and a blood-stained, half-naked corpse lying alone in a bare unfurnished room, should teach us a lesson, and we should profit by it.

The ex-Khedive a few years ago was " the modern Pharaoh," and no one could be loud enough in praise of " this enlightened prince." What is he now ?   An exile and an outcast.

We must at present, and until things are fashioned by degrees on the anvil of time, maintain the present government of Turkey ; but in return for that maintenance we have the right to insist—ay, and we must use that right—that in return for Lord Beaconsfield having saved the Turkish dominions from being utterly overrun and entirely destroyed by the Muscovite hordes, the territories still owning the sway of the Sultan, shall be justly and honestly administered. If the present state of Turkish finance is so bad that salaries of judges and gendarmes cannot be paid,

let us answer the question by appointing more
consular officers with an efficient staff, and as
John Bull has plenty of burdens to bear, say
frankly and openly to the Turks, "Whilst we
find it necessary to keep up this staff we shall do
so, and will pay for it out of the surplus revenue
of Cyprus, instead of handing it over to you;
when your administration is so improved that
the presence of these officers is no longer
necessary, we will withdraw them and pay you
the money."

Our absolute right to do this can be questioned
by no one; the June Convention imposed upon
the Turks the duty of reforming the many
abuses of their local administration and judicial
practice; this they have almost entirely neglected
to do, and therefore have voided their contract.
To say that, therefore, we are released from the
obligation to defend Asiatic Turkey is beside
the question; the Turk is clever enough to
know that our own interests will prevent our
acquiescing in the Russian possession of the
great highway of the past, and also of the

future, between the East and West, and therefore will do nothing.   Touch him in his pocket
and he will soon begin to move.

The Walis, Mutesarifs, Kaimacans, Mudirs,
and all the official hierarchy, when their power
of taking bribes is diminished, as it will be by
the supervision of English officers, will be
unable to fee the carrion crew that now batten
on the vitals of the empire, and the foul
herd, lacking sustenance, will be starved into
harmlessness.

In all these questions of reforms, the inter-
communication between the different provinces
and the provision of outlets for the produce
must be considered.   My own belief is " That
good communications mean good civilisation."
In Africa, in Asia, in America, as roads and
railways progress, as the means of communication are improved, so will barbarism, savagery,
heathenism and all the other evils of the hidden
corners of the earth die out before the light of
civilisation.   Some people say that it is better
for the natives of countries as yet untainted by

the vices and evils of modern civilisation to
retain the practice of their primitive customs
and habits, lest in searching for greater good
they lose the little they possess already. Civilisation and education may entail some evils,
but it is rarely, owing to our human imperfec-
tions, that we can find an unmixed good in this
world. No one will dare to deny that the
desire for more light which is so deeply rooted
in the human breast is not one of the divinest
attributes of our nature, and where long centuries of oppression and debasement have
caused this desire to wither and fade away,
nothing can be more truly deserving of praise
than efforts to cause this drooping plant to
revive.

The Mohammedan religion, which has performed, and in North Central Africa is still
performing, a great civilising and educational
function, has in the Sultan's dominions lost its
fructifying power, and leads to an apathy
amongst its professors which is the cause of
many of the evils we have to deplore. Though

the Mohammedan peasantry are sober, frugal,
and industrious, and constantly, if not usually,
superior to their fellow subjects of the same
rank who belong to other religions, still the
case of one of them rising to wealth and riches
is rare indeed.   The fatalist doctrines of Islam
cause them to be contented with whatever may
happen to them, and prevent their using the
smallest precaution to avert anticipated evil
or disaster.   Hardy, loyal, easily disciplined,
second to none in bravery, and patient under
trials and fatigues, they can be fashioned into
troops equal to the *élite* of Western Europe ;
but left to themselves, or without European
aid, we must not look to them to have sufficient
energy and *verve* to become great factors in the
reform of the East.

Though the Christians are more dishonest,
drunken, and generally untrustworthy (of course
there are many glorious exceptions) than their
Mohammedan neighbours, still they understand
that there is a higher and a better state of
existence in this world than that they drag out

at present, and therefore they eagerly accept
every scrap of education for their children, and
pinch and save to enable them to go to schools
and colleges whenever and wherever they have
the opportunity.

Of the two Christian races in Turkey which
occupy the foremost place, viz : the Greeks and
the Armenians, I should be inclined to place
more trust in the latter as being of importance
in the regeneration of the East.   Europe, in
freeing Greece, performed a worthy and a noble
action, but we must rid ourselves of the glamour
thrown over the Greek nation by the gorgeous
and graphic word-painting of the poet Byron,
and also by the remembrance of the great men
of old.

If we consider the number of years, centuries,
that it took to produce the literature and art of
the Greek nation, which we moderns, owing to
the way it is brought before us, focussed into a
point, are apt to regard as the outcome of a
glorious galaxy of talent, we shall see that far
more stupendous works are undertaken, more

beautiful pictures are painted, more literature
worthy of abiding to the latest time is written
in one year in England in the Victorian era
than was ever the case in the days of ancient
Greece. We speak of Demosthenes ; could his
most bitter philipics be greater specimens of
oratory than the speeches we are in the habit
of hearing from Beaconsfield, Gladstone, and
Bright ? In the second rank of orators we have
men who, when their day has passed by, will
be forgotten, who, if they had lived in classic
days, would have had their speeches handed
down as models of thought and style.

The Armenians (and other Christian races,
excluding the Greeks,) are not perhaps so quick
in their intelligence as the Greeks, but they
have more solid and enduring qualities, and are
not so entirely devoted to money-grubbing, and
so apt to consider all things fair in order to
attain the great end of getting rich quickly.
At Constantinople the Armenians have established a sort of private parliament, where
they discuss and settle matters pertaining to

themselves without asking any aid from government, and indeed raise money to carry out their decisions. This is a great step in the way of self-government, but unfortunately the Armenians are so mixed up with other races that it seems almost impossible to establish an Armenia which might be governed and administered by Armenians; and of course the whole nationality is not so far advanced as those who reside at Constantinople.

Native support must be given to all schemes of reforms, whether they consist in amendment of laws or in making of roads; and we must, in order to form our Future Highway, attract to our side to assist us the inhabitants of the countries through which it will pass. It may be well supposed, if we alleviate the sufferings of the Armenians, they in return will aid us in our desires.

There is just time and space here to notice an article in the *Fortnightly Review* by Mr. Blunt — "An Indo-Mediterranean Railway: Fiction and Fact." It is written in the most

kindly spirit imaginable, but instead of being
an argument against the establishment of the
railway along the line I have pointed out, it,
on the contrary, affords some of the strongest
reasons in its favour.

The only three arguments against it in the
article to which any weight could possibly be
attached, are, 1st, That India does not want
it; 2nd, That the country is not rich enough
to support it; 3rd, That it would be impossible
to restore, at all events in the present age, the
ancient productiveness of Babylonia and other
countries watered by the Tigris and Euphrates.

To the first it may be said that India did not
want the Overland Route, India did not want the
Suez Canal, India did not want railways, India
did not want roads, India did not want canals
—where would India be without all these at
the present day ? A new line of communication
which would not compete with the old ones,
but which would supplement them, and aid
them, would be of inestimable use, even although the Indian official mind is not ripe to

see it. They admit that Himalayan tea would
use this route; if it answered for Himalayan
tea, we should soon find other teas, coffee, indigo
and more valuable produce following the same
line. That the telegraph will always antici-
pate mails is true; but nevertheless the more
rapidly mails can be conveyed, the greater will
be the benefit to the official, the commercial,
and the social world. The Persian Gulf is
far cooler than the Red Sea for the greater
portion of the year, and the months in which it
is hotter are those in which no one goes out to
or returns from India, unless forced to do so.

2nd. That the country is not rich enough
to support a line down the Euphrates I quite
admit; all armies that advanced by the line of
the Euphrates, notably those of Cyrus and
Julian, were dependent on their accompanying flotillas for their commissariat, and without
them would have been helpless.

Consular reports are too long to quote, and
masses of figures convey little idea to the mind,
but those who care for statistics may study

them with advantage, and will, I am certain
be convinced that the country not only is
much richer at present than it is supposed to
be, notwithstanding its mal-government, but
that its comparative poverty arises chiefly from
the want of proper means of communications.

3rd. The ancient productiveness of the
country still remains; the canals of which
Mr. Blunt speaks were principally strategical
works, and not primarily intended for the
irrigation of the country. Indian irrigation
is not a parallel case, and where one scheme
has failed, as some have, through the bur-
den of officialism it has had to bear, many
others have survived and prospered in spite
of it.

But irrigation of the lands along the Tigris
need not be so expensive as those in India;
a turbine pump here and there driven by the
current would serve to raise water to any
requisite height, and it could be distributed to
any distance by means of cast-iron pipes, which
cost little or nothing more than pig-iron.

9 783348 054072